To be desired by someone strong... six years younger than her...

She pulled away suddenly and grabbed hold of the counter for support. What had she been thinking? Logan had agreed to help her with the renovation; he'd let her dump her family problems on him like a real friend. But it couldn't be more than that. They both knew it. She couldn't bear to take this any further and have him disappointed. Somehow she knew being rejected by Logan would be a million times worse than her own husband's betrayal.

"I'm—" she began.

"Don't apologize," he said, his breathing as uneven as hers.

"I took advantage of you," she countered.

He let out a harsh bark of laughter. "I kissed *you*, Olivia."

"Because you felt sorry for me."

"Because I wanted to kiss you." He pushed a hand through his blond hair, tousling it in a way that made her want to brush it back into place. Because at her core, Olivia liked things in their place, even if that place kept her lonely and afraid. She didn't think she had the guts to live life any other way.

Dear Reader,

I'm so happy to welcome you back to Crimson, Colorado, a small town nestled in the beautiful Rocky Mountains. To me it's the perfect place to fall in love.

Unfortunately, Olivia Wilder hasn't been too lucky in Crimson. Her husband, the town's mayor, cheated, then left her with a pile of debt and humiliation. But during her short time there, Olivia has already fallen in love with the small mountain community and is determined to make a home in Crimson while protecting her heart against any more pain.

Logan Travers never expected to return to his hometown. A family tragedy left him wild, reckless and only able to find some sense of peace once he left Crimson. But a chance encounter with Olivia makes him wonder if the future he craves might be found in Crimson after all.

Olivia and Logan are opposites in every way except how love might help them heal their hearts if they can risk enough to be together.

I hope you enjoy their story and look for more books coming from Crimson this year. I love to hear from readers at michelle@michellemajor.com.

Best,

Michelle Major

A Second Chance at Crimson Ranch

Michelle Major

HARLEQUIN® SPECIAL EDITION®

Recycling programs
for this product may
not exist in your area.

ISBN-13: 978-0-373-65873-2

A Second Chance at Crimson Ranch

Copyright © 2015 by Michelle Major

Printed in U.S.A.

Michelle Major grew up in Ohio but dreamed of living in the mountains. Soon after graduating with a degree in journalism, she pointed her car west and settled in Colorado. Her life and house are filled with one great husband, two beautiful kids, a few furry pets and several well-behaved reptiles. She's grateful to have found her passion writing stories with happy endings. Michelle loves to hear from her readers at michellemajor.com.

Books by Michelle Major

Harlequin Special Edition

A Kiss on Crimson Ranch
A Brevia Beginning
Her Accidental Engagement
Still the One

Visit the Author Profile page at Harlequin.com for more titles.

To my daughter, Jessie, who makes me smile every day. I love you to the moon and back a gazillion times and can't wait to watch you make all your dreams come true.

Chapter One

Olivia Wilder loved weddings, even if she no longer believed in marriage. At least not for herself.

She wasn't one to let her personal prejudice ruin someone else's happiness. Especially someone who deserved it as much as her friend Sara Wellens—Sara Travers as of two hours ago.

But the champagne Olivia had drained during the toast was doing funny things to her brain. Her hand fluttered in front of her face as she blinked back tears.

"Tears of joy," she assured Sara, who looked at her with a mix of understanding and sympathy that made Olivia want to cry harder. "I'm thrilled for you and Josh."

"I know, sweetie." Sara gave her a gentle hug. They'd become close friends during the past six months. "And you're better off without that slimeball husband anyway."

Olivia nodded. "You're one of the lucky ones. Josh is a great guy. He loves you to the ends of the earth." She hiccupped. "Nothing like Craig."

"Craig was a loser." Olivia couldn't help but smile at Sara's blunt description.

"And a cheater." Olivia looked over Sara's shoulder to where their friend Natalie Holt sat perched at the edge of the couch in the ladies' lounge. The three of them had escaped into the private room for a few minutes to help Sara get ready to leave for her honeymoon. "He's going to be sorry he didn't do right by you. You were the best thing that ever happened to him."

Natalie was another friend Olivia had met in Crimson, Colorado, the town her soon-to-be ex-husband had become mayor of right after they'd married. That had been almost two years ago. From the start, Olivia had loved the small mountain town, felt at home there in a way she never had growing up in Saint Louis or at college on the East Coast. Craig had said it was only the first stop on his political career, although she would have been happy living in Crimson forever.

Now she knew she'd never get that chance.

"We shouldn't be wallowing in my sad story." Olivia made her voice light as she drew away from Sara. "This day is about you and that hot new husband of yours."

A dreamy smile lit up Sara's face. "He's pretty cute, huh?"

Natalie laughed. "Puppies and rainbows are cute. Josh Travers is one hundred proof stud. Even I'd brave the flight to Hawaii just to watch him on the beach for a week."

Olivia smiled, knowing Natalie was petrified of airplanes. "Are you ready to go? Bags all packed?" Olivia asked. Sara and Josh were driving to Denver after the reception and flying out in the morning.

Sara pointed to a mini suitcase in the corner. "I've got everything I need."

Olivia felt her eyes widen. "That's all you're taking for a week away?"

Craig had insisted on a fancy cruise for their honeymoon, and she'd had to bring two huge suitcases to accommodate all the clothes she'd needed for dinners, parties and the like.

"Sara won't need more than a bikini," Natalie said with a knowing smile. "And Josh will probably have her out of that most of the time anyway."

"I sure hope so." Sara winked then shook her head at Olivia's expression. "You're blushing, Olivia."

"I don't know...yes...well..."

Natalie gave an indelicate snort. "Was Craig such a limp fish even on the honeymoon? It's not a surprise, but still..."

Olivia shrugged. "It was fine." But nothing about her relationship with Craig had been fine, including their honeymoon. She knew she was to blame for that as well, or at least that's what he'd convinced her at the time.

She busied herself with folding Sara's bridal veil before carefully placing it in the box.

"You won't leave before I get back?" Sara's voice was so soft it made Olivia's eyes prick again.

"Why do you have to leave at all?" Natalie asked, rising to stand next to Sara. "You love it in Crimson. This town is great for you."

She smiled slightly at Natalie's indignant tone. It had been so long—forever really—since Olivia had felt like she had friends in her corner. "Craig ruined both our reputations. Even if I had the money to stay, I doubt I'd feel at home here anymore."

"He was the dirty, cheating scumbag. Not you."

"You know how things work in a small town."

Natalie's lips thinned into a frustrated line and she flipped a strand of soft caramel-colored hair behind her shoulder. She'd grown up in Crimson and knew better than any of them about life in a small town. "The best things about Crimson are also the hardest," she said. "Always have been. People here are ready to help someone in need at the drop of a hat, but they also want to learn all your business in the process."

"People in town mean well. You know they do." Sara wrapped an arm around Natalie's shoulder. "Even if your trust tree has very few branches. We all know you like to keep your secrets even closer than your friends."

"I don't have secrets, you brat," Natalie answered with a grin. She gave Sara a playful flick on her bare shoulder. "I'm an open book and everyone knows it."

As both women erupted into laughter, a subtle ache started in Olivia's chest. In her ivory gown, Sara, a blonde-haired, blue-eyed beauty, looked every bit as ready to walk the red carpet as when she actually would for a movie premier. The turquoise necklace bright against her fair skin and the cowboy boots she wore with her wedding dress were the only things that gave a hint to the work she did running the guest ranch nestled at the base of the mountains outside of town.

Natalie was a good six inches shorter than Olivia, her light brown hair and matching eyes warm and kind. But the faint shadows under her eyes proved that Natalie worked too hard balancing her jobs as a nurse at the local retirement home and a part-time private caretaker.

Along with Sara's long-time friend April, these two women had become the sisters Olivia had always longed to have. They'd accepted and supported her, pulled her out of her rigid shell and were teaching her how to enjoy life.

She'd almost been happy until Craig had walked out

on her two months ago, taking her life savings and her self-respect along with him.

But that was too maudlin a topic for a night such as this. She plastered a bright smile on her face. "No more depressing Craig talk. Let's get back out there and join the party."

Sara pointed a finger at her. "You need a man," she said, ignoring Olivia's fake smile.

"Josh has two brothers," Natalie offered.

"I don't need a man," Olivia sputtered, feeling heat rise to her cheeks again. "I just got rid of one."

"Craig was a snake, not a man." Sara waved a dismissive hand. "He doesn't count. Josh's brothers aren't staying in town long enough to be useful. Plus, Jake said he's due back at the clinic by Tuesday morning. Logan is too much of a wild card to depend on."

"What about—" Natalie started.

Olivia threw up her hands. "Stop!"

Both women turned to her. "I'm not looking for a man," she repeated.

"You're in a bad place," Natalie argued. "You need to let loose."

"My husband left, taking most of my money with him. Heck, yeah, I'm in a bad place." Olivia placed her hands on her hips and narrowed her gaze at Natalie. "I'm not the only one who needs to let loose. How about we find a man for you?"

Natalie's shoulders stiffened. "This isn't about me."

"We just want you to stay," Sara said softly.

"I know." The tension went out of Olivia's shoulders. She wanted the same thing. She just couldn't figure out how to make it happen. "I won't leave until you get back. I'm meeting with the new mayor this week. Maybe I'll have some great epiphany before then."

A knock sounded on the door and Josh Travers walked in.

"Hello, husband," Sara said, her dreamy smile returning.

"Hello, wife," he answered and came forward to wrap her in his arms. "The guests are asking for you." He nodded at Natalie and Olivia. "Mind if I have a few moments with her, ladies?"

"Of course not," Olivia and Natalie answered in unison.

"Come on, Livvy," Natalie said with a smile. "Let's round up a couple more glasses of champagne."

Sara touched Olivia's arm as she walked past. "You deserve happiness, too," she whispered.

Olivia's throat clogged, but she nodded and then followed Natalie back to the reception.

Logan Travers tipped the beer bottle to his lips as he scanned the guests at the reception. They'd sent off Josh and Sara half an hour ago in a flurry of well wishes and whistles, but the absence of the bride and groom hadn't seemed to dampen the party atmosphere in the least. He was happy for Josh, and Sara seemed amazing, but that didn't mean he liked wedding receptions.

He curled two fingers into his collar and tried to stretch the starched fabric. This was the first time in his life he'd worn a tuxedo, and he hoped it would be the last. He was ready to head back to Josh's ranch and crawl into bed for the night. His brother Jake had left already, using the fact that he was driving Josh's daughter, Claire, home as an excuse. Logan figured it had more to do with Jake's need to get away from the boisterous crowd drinking and dancing in the private reception hall above one of Crimson's popular downtown restaurants.

Logan had been close to making his own escape, but

his new sister-in-law had cornered him on her way out and made him promise to dance with one of her single friends before he left. He'd worked his butt off all night to avoid getting entangled with any of the women at the wedding, limiting his dancing to his thirteen-year-old niece. But he'd been unable to resist Sara's plea.

Now he surveyed the couples on the dance floor and the people scattered at tables around the room. His eye caught on a woman seated by herself to the side of the dance floor. She looked as uncomfortable as he felt. Her dress was pale pink and her hair was pulled back from her face in an almost severe knot at the back of her head. Sara had described her friend Olivia as a very pretty librarian type. Logan didn't know if he agreed with that, but decided she must be the woman.

As he approached her, the music changed to a slow ballad. Damn. He'd been hoping to make it through some hokey line dance with her and call it good. He thought about ducking away, but her gaze lifted to his so there was no turning back.

"Would you care to dance?" he asked, stretching out his hand, palm up.

She eyed his fingers as if they were spikes on a cactus. "Why are you asking?"

He hadn't expected her question. Logan couldn't remember the last time—if ever—a woman had offered any resistance to his interest in her. One side of his mouth lifted. "We're at a wedding. There's music." He took a step closer and brought his hand to his hip. "I'm Logan Travers, Josh's brother."

Her big gray eyes flicked to his before returning to the dance floor. "I know who you are, and I'm guessing Sara put you up to this."

He didn't bother to deny it. "I don't know her well, but she's pretty insistent when she wants something."

"They've left," the woman answered tonelessly. "You're off the hook."

That was exactly what he'd wanted mere minutes ago, but now he felt like he was getting the brush-off. "You don't think she'll be looking for a report after the honeymoon?"

"You seem to know Sara better than you think." Her mouth curved into a genuine smile. Logan lifted his hand to his collar again, unable to explain the heat that shot through his spine. The woman stood and he was surprised at her height, especially since her shoes had very little heel.

She was nowhere near as tall as he was, but at six-foot-three he was used to towering over most people. She was just a slip of a thing but only had to tip her head a bit to look him in the eye. Suddenly he wanted nothing more than to take her in his arms and discover if she'd fit there as well as he thought she would.

"I'm Olivia," she said and extended her hand.

He covered her fingers in his and tugged her toward the dance floor.

"You don't have to do this," she protested.

"I want to." He pulled her into his arms, maybe a bit closer than was necessary.

Automatically, her left hand came to rest on his shoulder as he kept her right one wrapped in his. He couldn't help but notice the enormous diamond on her ring finger. He was almost blinded as it caught the light. Sara had asked him to dance with her single friend, but the ring meant there was more to the story.

He tried to ignore his curiosity as his fingers brushed the gauzy fabric of her dress along her back. A few pieces of mahogany-colored hair fell loose against her neck and he reveled in their softness as the strands grazed his cheek. She smelled like flowers, and he resisted the urge to bury his face in the crook of her neck and breathe in the fragrance.

He gave himself a few moments to regain his control. Clearly he'd been too long without the company of a woman based on his body's reaction to Olivia. She wasn't his type in any way. She was too refined, too fragile, too reserved. Logan liked his female companions loud and fun. He was in it for a down-and-dirty good time. Everything about Olivia screamed *out of your league*. He was smart enough to believe it.

"Why don't you have a date?" he couldn't help asking.

He felt her body stiffen but her voice was calm when she answered. "My husband was a serial cheater who ran off with his secretary a few months ago."

His step almost faltered at her blunt honesty. He leaned back to look into her eyes. "Then he didn't deserve you in the first place," he told her quietly.

Her breath hitched as her mouth formed a perfect O. There was a bleakness in her gaze, a quiet desperation that Logan hadn't seen in a woman since he'd looked into his twin sister's eyes almost ten years ago. Olivia Wilder was broken, he realized. He didn't know her husband, but had the fierce desire to plow his fist into the other man's jaw.

"He wanted to discover his bliss," she said after a minute. "The life we had was stifling for him."

"Tell me you're not defending the jerk."

She shook her head but her eyes dropped to his bow tie. "It will be better in the long run."

"Is that what he told you?"

"It's what I tell myself to get through each day," she answered then blinked, her eyes filling with tears.

The music ended and she pulled away, but he held on to her hand. "Let's get a beer."

She shook her head as if realizing she'd revealed too much but followed as he led her off the dance floor toward the bar. He could feel the weight of the stares from the other guests. He hadn't stepped foot in Crimson in close to a decade and saw no point in making friends during this return trip. He planned to get the hell out of town as soon as Josh and Sara returned from Hawaii.

Without letting go of Olivia's hand, he grabbed two beers from the bartender and made a path toward the hallway that led to the stairs by the main restaurant. He wanted to head outside, but he knew it was too cold for her in that thin dress. It was late March and at the nine-thousand-foot altitude where Crimson sat nestled in a valley high in the Rocky Mountains of Colorado, the temperature at night was still below freezing.

Instead, he took her to the back of the restaurant, which was empty so late on a Saturday night. He pulled out a chair and she sank down, cradling her head in her hands as her shoulders shook.

"Go away," she mumbled between her fingers.

Logan opened the beer bottles and sat one on the table in front of her. "Drink this."

He took a long pull on his, then ran a hand through his hair.

"I prefer white wine," she told him, her voice still shaky.

"I'm fresh out," he answered and she raised her head to glare at him, wiping the tips of her long fingers across her cheeks. Good. Anger he could deal with a lot easier than sorrow.

"You don't want them to see you hurting. They'll take too much interest in it. That's how small towns work." He took several paces across the empty dining room, wondering why this woman's sadness bothered him so much. Wondering if his advice was more for her or himself.

"Everyone in Crimson has been great to me since I arrived." She took a sip of the beer, made a face and then swallowed another bigger drink. "Besides, I *am* hurting. My husband was mayor of Crimson. I had a very public image in this town. We had the perfect life. Now I look like a fool."

"I'm not going to argue about your version of the *perfect life*. The fact that he cheated, then left you is his problem, not yours."

"It's mine when he left with all of my money and hadn't paid our mortgage in months. He left me with nothing." She clapped a hand over her mouth. "You don't want to hear about my problems."

"Don't be too sure. Who was this pillar of the community?"

She picked at one corner of the bottle's label. "Craig Wilder. He comes from a prominent family in Crimson."

Logan felt his jaw clench. "I know who the Wilders are."

"Were you friends with Craig growing up?"

He almost laughed at that one. "He went to school with my oldest brother."

Her gaze became speculative. "How old are you, Logan?"

"Twenty-six."

"A baby," she whispered.

"Hardly," he countered. "So what's your plan now?"

She took another drink of beer. "I don't have one. I was working on renovating the community center downtown, but it was in a volunteer capacity. I think Craig mainly gave me the job to keep me busy and unaware of his extracurricular activities. I'm not sure what happens now. The contractor heading up the remodeling was the husband of Craig's mistress. Needless to say, I don't think he's too excited about a project that helps the town."

"But what happens with you?"

"My mom still lives in Saint Louis, where I grew up. I'm going to stay with her and regroup."

"What about the community center?"

She sat the beer bottle on the table and wrapped her arms around her waist. "It would have been good for Crimson. I had so many plans: art classes, events, reviving the theater, workshops for seniors. We were going to bring together people of all generations and walks of life in Crimson. The center would have highlighted local artists and brought guest teachers to the area. It had so much potential."

For the first time, Logan saw something more than disappointment in her gaze. When she talked about the community center, it was with passion and dedication.

"It still does," he answered.

Her eyes searched his as if she expected to see something he knew she'd never find. She stood and took a step toward him as if drawn by the same invisible connection he was having trouble ignoring. "Why do you care about this?"

"I don't." He took a drink of beer and looked away. "I'm making conversation to stop you from crying." He forced his lips into a casual smile. "I've been away from Crimson for a while, but I've still got a reputation to protect. One dance with me and a woman bursts into tears. I don't think so."

That made her smile and the strange charge between

them disappeared. "I'll be sure to tell everyone how that one dance was an amazing, life-altering moment for me."

He didn't know whether to laugh or be offended at her sarcasm. Before he could decide, she lifted onto her toes and brushed a quick kiss across his cheek. "It was nice meeting you, Logan. Thank you for the dance," she said softly. "I owe Sara for making you ask me."

"My sister-in-law didn't make me do anything." Suddenly it was important Olivia understand that fact.

She only smiled over her shoulder and walked out of the restaurant.

Logan sank into her chair after she'd gone. Her perfume still lingered in the air and he closed his eyes to focus on the expensive floral scent. He'd been back in Crimson for less than a week, enough time to reconnect with his brothers and attend Josh and Sara's wedding. But already he felt his equilibrium shifting. His reaction to Olivia Wilder tonight was proof of that.

He needed to get back to his regular life sooner rather than later, which wouldn't involve an extended stay in his hometown. He'd left that chapter of his life behind long ago.

Chapter Two

Olivia nervously tapped her toe on the floor as she waited in the lobby outside the mayor's office two days later. She tried to relax, to think of flowery meadows and golden light, but the only image that popped into her mind was Logan Travers's face as she'd kissed him. As silly as it was, she could still feel the rough stubble of his cheek and smell the woodsy, all-male scent of him. What had possessed her to kiss him as she'd walked away after the reception?

As innocent as it had been, Olivia had never done anything so forward in her life. Put her mouth on a practical stranger, even a tiny peck. She almost giggled at the absurdly liberating feeling it gave her, which at least served to calm her nerves a bit.

To him it had probably meant nothing, much like their one dance. He'd been fulfilling an obligation, end of story. Olivia certainly knew a lot about being an obligation.

No more. That wasn't how she'd live her life going forward.

"Marshall will see you now." The new assistant eyed her with a mix of curiosity and sympathy.

"Thank you," Olivia answered and, her nerves fluttering, walked into the office her husband had occupied only months ago.

Marshall Daley looked at home behind the desk she'd come to think of as Craig's. He'd been appointed mayor pro tem after Craig resigned and would complete her husband's term until the next election. Marshall was a lifelong resident of Crimson, a retired insurance salesman and Olivia knew he'd do the right thing for the town as mayor.

She closed the door and took a seat across from him. "How are things going?"

He sat back and drew in a long breath. "They'd be a hell of a lot better if your husband hadn't run off, leaving his responsibilities floating in the breeze."

"Ex-husband," she clarified. "Almost. I've got another few weeks before the divorce is final."

"And you've heard nothing from him?"

She shook her head.

"I was so sure he'd come home and make this right." Marshall picked up a pen from the desk and twirled it absently between his fingers.

"My soon-to-be ex-husband is a selfish jerk who doesn't care about right or wrong. *My* concern is what happens to the community center after this."

She felt herself twisting her wedding ring around her finger, still keeping up appearances despite the fact that her marriage had been a disaster. A part of her had, like Marshall, held out hope Craig would make things right and save her from looking like the fool she was. A look of pity crossed Marshall's face, making her want to run shrieking from the building. She tried to see herself through the new mayor's eyes. She'd worn a business suit to the meeting, the kind she normally reserved for town meetings. Now the tailored gray wool felt tight and itchy, as if it didn't belong against her skin, the same way she no longer fit the mold of complacent political wife.

"Unfortunately, the community center may become one more casualty of Craig's abandonment." Marshall shrugged. "Jeremy Dempsey wants nothing to do with the renovations. You must have noticed that work has stopped on the project."

She nodded. She'd driven by the job site on the way to this meeting, disappointed to see the darkened building.

"Without a general contractor, the work is stalled indefinitely. We can't find anyone willing to take over. Guys feel like they're being disloyal to Jeremy if they even return my calls. It's like he wants to punish the town for Craig and Melissa's misdeeds."

Olivia had heard that Jeremy was making things difficult around town since learning his wife was Craig's mistress. Olivia understood all too well the humiliation, hurt and anger Jeremy probably felt. "It's not right that the people of Crimson should be punished. Craig and Melissa had hardly anything to do with the community center. I swear the only reason either of them cared about it was because it kept Jeremy and me occupied and off their trail."

"I understand that," Marshall said with a slight cringe. "I also know how hard you worked on the project, and I agree that the town needs it. But there's no one in Crimson willing to take over, Olivia. I'll have a public relations nightmare on my hands if I hire someone from out of town. I'm putting out a dozen fires as it is thanks to all the things Craig left undone."

"You can't give up on this," she argued.

"We need more money to finish the project. I know you did the initial fund-raising when you were the mayor's wife, but things have changed." He sighed and rubbed two thick fingers against his forehead. "There's a real estate developer who's interested in the building. He wants to turn the space into condos."

"No!" Olivia felt her heart pound against her rib cage. She'd worked hard to convince Craig to support the community center. She had so many plans for it and couldn't stand to see them circling the drain this way.

Marshall started at her outburst, then shrugged. "I'm sorry, Olivia. I don't have a choice."

She wasn't sure what she'd expected from this meeting. A part of her had hoped Marshall would say the community center could be saved. That would at least allow her to leave Crimson knowing she'd done some good during her time here. "What if I continue fund-raising?" she offered suddenly. "I've been managing most of the work anyway."

"I thought you were moving back to Missouri?"

She pressed her lips together as indecision filled her. That had been the plan, the easiest way to leave behind this humiliating chapter of her life. The past two months had been awful. Olivia had hardly left her house other than to visit the ranch or Natalie's small apartment. She drove to a town forty-five minutes away to do her grocery shopping so no one would stop her in the aisles. She knew people meant well, but she couldn't stand how stupid she felt after being duped and then dumped by her husband.

Sara's wedding had been the first time she'd been out in public since Craig's departure. There she'd ended up sulking at a table before crying on a stranger's shoulder on the dance floor. Not the most stellar re-entry into the community.

A vision of Logan's piercing blue eyes came to mind. She thought about his comment that Craig's leaving wasn't her fault. She may not agree. but it was time to stop cowering behind closed doors. She loved the town of Crimson and the friends she'd made here. Why should her lying, cheating, rat husband rob her of this place, too?

She straightened her shoulders and met Marshall's gaze across the desk. "I'd like to stay and see the community center open. Like you said, the town needs it." She paused then added, "I need it."

"I don't know if continuing to keep this project going will help either of us at this point."

She leaned forward the tiniest bit. "I'm not the only one whose reputation has suffered from Craig's leaving. I know the mayor's office is under a lot of scrutiny. You need some positive press for the town, especially before tourist season starts. The center was set to open by early May. I can still deliver that date. I'll talk to Jeremy and convince him to keep working on the project. Or I'll find someone to replace him."

His bushy eyebrows rose. "That's aggressive, Olivia."

"It's time I got aggressive about something, Marshall."

He studied her for a few moments, then nodded. "If you want a salary, you'll have to come up with grant money to cover it. I know you did everything as a volunteer when you were the mayor's wife, but I can't start paying you now."

"Don't worry," she assured him with more confidence than she felt. "I can take care of myself."

There's a first time for everything.

He looked as if he wanted to argue, but she stood be-

fore he could speak. "You won't regret this. I promise."
She extended her hand and he shook it tentatively.

"I hope you're right," he said.

Me, too, she added silently.

She turned to leave.

"Olivia?"

Marshall's voice stopped her as she reached for the
door. She turned.

"You were too good for him from the start," he told
her.

"Thank you," she whispered, swallowing down her
emotions.

Without looking back again, she walked out of the
town hall and into her new life.

"You're not being fair," Olivia argued later that week.

She stood in the back of Crimson's local building-and-
supply store, where she'd cornered Jeremy Dempsey after
he'd repeatedly ignored her calls.

"The town was weeks behind on our payment schedule."

"There was a lot of turmoil after Craig and Melissa
left, but we've straightened things out. You've been paid
now." Olivia had watched the finance manager cut the
check herself.

"Who's to say it won't happen again?" Jeremy turned
away and grabbed a box from the shelf.

"I know this isn't about the money. The community
center will help the town in so many different ways. Don't
let your personal feelings cloud your judgment this way."

He gave her a once over. "Since when did you become
the town champion?"

"I'm learning to be my own champion. Marshall put

me in charge of the project." That stretched the truth, but Olivia had to prove she could do this.

"Not good enough," he told her. "Your husband is a two-timing, lousy—"

"Ex-husband," she corrected. "Soon to be, anyway. Trust me, I know every one of Craig's shortcomings and I'm sorry for what he did. What both he and your wife did. But I shouldn't be punished for his sins. This town needs the community center. I want to make things right."

"You could have made things right by keeping Craig's wandering eye on you." His eyes blazed as he spat out the words. "Maybe if he'd been happy at home, none of this would have happened."

Olivia took a step back as if he'd slapped her. She knew Jeremy had a son who was now without his mother. Olivia wasn't the only one who'd been wronged, nor was hers the biggest loss. She'd been trying to convince herself that it wasn't her fault. Jeremy's angry words echoed in her head. If Craig had been more interested in her, maybe none of this would have happened.

She sucked in a breath at the thought.

This was hopeless. What had made her think she could extricate herself from the shadow of Craig's deception and make a home in this town? She didn't belong in Crimson.

Emotions flooded her and she turned to flee, only to run into someone. Someone tall and extremely solid. She glanced up to find Logan Travers staring down at her. She saw a look of understanding pass through his eyes and nearly groaned. Of course he would have heard the accusation Jeremy had thrown at her. She wondered briefly if it was possible to actually die of embarrassment.

His hands felt warm on her arms as he set her back a few steps. "You're not running," he whispered, then raised his head to greet Jeremy. "It's been a while, Jeremy. How are things?"

The other man's gaze swung between her and Logan, clearly trying to come up with a connection. "I'm getting by," Jeremy answered. "I'm surprised to see you back in town, Travers. With the way things were going, I figured you'd have ended up in jail by now."

Olivia's breath caught at the blatant rudeness of the words.

Logan didn't seem to mind. One corner of his mouth lifted. "I turned things around. It happens."

"Construction attracts all types. Lots of guys just hanging on to the edges of the business to stay afloat." Jeremy gave a jerky nod. "I hear you're building houses in Telluride."

"Things are good down there. I've been lucky with the people I've gotten to know. Some builders care about doing things right. Others cut corners wherever they can." His blue eyes met Olivia's gaze. "I stopped by the community center building the other day. There are some problems with the wiring and insulation you're going to want fixed before you continue."

Jeremy took a step forward. "Are you hinting that those problems are my fault?"

Logan shrugged. "I'm saying it's important to get the right people working on the project."

"You've got some nerve, Travers." Jeremy Dempsey's temper was back in full force. "I remember when you were a scrawny kid running wild around this town. You and your sister raising holy hell all over the place."

"A lot has changed since then," Logan answered casually but Olivia saw a muscle tick in his jaw.

Jeremy must have realized he'd stepped over some invisible line because his attention turned to Olivia. "I don't want anything to do with your project and I'll make sure no other contractor in Crimson will, either."

"It's a community center *for* Crimson," she said, trying not to sound as desperate as she felt. "I'm doing this to help the town."

"You could help by leaving," Jeremy said. "No one here needs the reminder of anyone or anything associated with Craig Wilder."

He turned on his heel and stomped off toward the front of the store.

She would have gone after him but Logan's hand clamped around her wrist. "You're better off without his help."

She shook off his grasp. "Easy for you to say. I need a contractor. I can't exactly renovate the building on my own."

An older man walked into their aisle, took something from the shelf and turned away without making eye contact. Great. She wondered how many people had overheard her argument with Jeremy. She'd never liked the guy but knew he was well-connected in the community.

She'd been running on adrenaline since her meeting at the mayor's office earlier in the week, but now her shoulders slumped under the weight of the task before her. She felt Logan's searching gaze and bit down on her lower lip. "I'm not going to lose it," she assured him.

He didn't look convinced. "Let me buy you a cup of coffee while we talk."

"I think you've done plenty of talking this morning." She walked past him up the aisle and out of the store, ignoring the stares from the men at the front counter.

To her surprise, Logan followed her down the street. Although it was sunny and clear, the air was still frigid and a layer of packed snow covered the streets.

"I'm sorry, Olivia," he said when she stopped at her Mercedes SUV. He turned her to look at him. His broad shoulders blocked the sun, but its reflection shone in his blond hair and highlighted his strong features and jaw line.

He was so handsome in broad daylight. It was a little difficult for Olivia to meet his gaze. She'd never been comfortable around really masculine men. The alpha type was far too intimidating. And everything about Logan screamed alpha male to her.

"It's fine," she mumbled, dropping her gaze to the sidewalk.

"I did go to the building site," he told her.

"Why?" she asked. "What does the community center matter to you?"

"I have an interest in design. I like to work on renovations rather than new construction, especially historic buildings. I have a few more days in town and it made me curious."

"And you found problems?"

"Nothing huge or structural." He shrugged. "I don't think Jeremy was doing his best work. You can find someone better. This is the slow season in construction. Lots of guys should have the time to fit this in."

She kicked her boot against a pile of dingy snow at the curb. "Not likely now." She paused as an idea struck her. "Unless you take over the construction."

So much for avoiding alpha males.

"No way," he answered quickly.

"Why not?" she countered, raising her gaze to meet his. "Jeremy isn't going to come back on the project, and who knows how long it will take to find another contractor. With the tight timeline, I need someone I can count on."

"What makes you think you can count on me?" His expression was guarded as he studied her.

It was crazy but the longer she thought about it, the more Olivia was convinced Logan could help her. That maybe he was the only person she could trust right now. "You're Josh's brother. I know he would vouch for you. That's a pretty strong reference."

"You heard Jeremy. My reputation in Crimson isn't the best."

"We all make mistakes."

"Mistakes," he repeated, laughing softly. "Right." He looked past her to where the mountains sat in the distance. Olivia loved those mountains and realized she'd do whatever she had to do to stay living in their shadow. "I left here a long time ago. This isn't my home anymore."

"You just said it's a slow season for construction. The whole thing should be finished in six weeks. There's an apartment over my garage that's empty. You can stay there."

"You don't know me well enough to offer me a job and a place to live."

"The fact that I don't know you is why I need you to take this job. You won't be affected by the gossip." As a brisk wind whipped down the street, Olivia started to zip up her puffer jacket, but it got caught in the fabric. She struggled with it as she spoke. "You saw how Jeremy treated me, how those men in the store looked at me. I'm quite the topic of conversation in certain circles these days. Most people are supportive, but for others it's my fault that Craig had a wandering eye. I don't like it and I don't want it to detract from the community center. You're the only person outside of my small group of friends who doesn't look at me with pity." She pulled harder on her coat, embarrassed that her fingers shook slightly. Glancing up at him, she said, "I can't take any more pity in my life, Logan."

His mouth opened as if he would argue but then shut again. He took a few quick steps away from where they stood, then stalked back. "This is a bad idea." He reached out to brush her hands aside. His long fingers gently worked the zipper free of the snag. He zipped up the coat to her chin, his knuckles grazing her jaw as he finished.

"But you'll do it," she suggested, her voice the tiniest bit breathless.

"I never was known for my good judgment," he answered. "Yes, I'll help you."

"You won't regret it. I promise." She smiled despite her nerves. "Would you be more comfortable staying with Josh and Sara? I'm sure they would—"

"The apartment is fine," he interrupted. "At the ranch I'll only be in the way. I need to drive down to Telluride for a few days and wrap up some loose ends. My roommate can take care of the house while I'm gone."

Roommate? Olivia couldn't help but wonder if that person was a woman or man. None of her concern. This arrangement was strictly business. She knew without a doubt that Logan Travers was too much for her.

Too attractive, too young, too dangerous.

Still, she felt relieved to have him working on the renovations with her. Something deep inside her relaxed with the knowledge that she wasn't alone on this project. She tried to convince herself it was simply having a contractor to handle the construction, but a part of her knew it had more to do with the man standing before her.

She took her cell phone from her purse and handed it to him. "Put your number in and I'll text you my address. I have some things to take care of in Denver over the weekend. We could meet at my house Monday morning, and I'll show you the plans and where we are on the project. You can get moved in, then we'll go from there."

He watched her for several long moments, those ice-blue eyes giving nothing away. "Are you sure this is what you want?" he asked finally.

I have no idea what I want, Olivia thought silently. Her plan was crazy, impulsive and the exact opposite behavior anyone would expect from Olivia Wilder.

"I'm positive," she answered.

Chapter Three

The following Monday, Logan let himself into the building at the edge of town that soon would house the community center Olivia was working so hard to make happen. There was no lock on the front door, something he planned to change today. Although the rooms were still under construction and unusable, he didn't believe in taking any chances.

As if in answer to his concerns, he heard a sound coming from the far end of the building. He made his way through the early morning shadows, careful not to make any noise as he walked.

The glow of a flashlight was visible in the large room that occupied the back half of the first floor. He stepped through and realized he needn't have worried about noise. The preteen boy who was currently spray painting a large B on the wall wore headphones. Logan could hear the bass echo in the empty space. The kid wore a flannel hoodie and jeans that rode low on his narrow hips. His dark brown hair was sleep tousled as he concentrated on his task.

When the boy started on an *i*, it was clear where the graffiti was headed. Wordlessly, Logan approached from behind, grabbing the hood of the boy's sweatshirt with one hand and ripping the headphones off with the other.

"What do you think you're doing, punk?"

The kid flailed, arms and legs flying as he tried to fight his way out of Logan's grasp. Logan figured he had more than a foot plus a good fifty pounds on the boy. It wasn't difficult to capture his wrists before shoving him into the wall.

"L-let go of me," the boy yelled.

"Not until you answer my question."

"What's it look like?" The kid's tone was surprisingly belligerent, but Logan felt a tremor of fear slide down his arms. "I'm sending a message."

"Who's it for?" Logan asked, although he could guess the answer.

"Olivia Wilder," the kid said with a sneer. "She's the biggest bi—"

"Watch it," Logan cautioned, pressing the boy a little harder against the wall. "She happens to be a friend of mine. What's your beef with Olivia?"

The boy's thin shoulders tensed and he was silent so long that Logan thought he might not answer. "My mom took off with her husband," the kid finally mumbled. He deflated so suddenly, Logan had to practically hold him up so he didn't sink to the floor.

Logan sighed as the situation became clear. "What's your name?"

"Jordan." The answer came through gritted teeth.

"How old are you, Jordan?"

"I'll be thirteen in two weeks."

"Jordan, I'm going to let go of your wrists now so we can talk man-to-man. But I'm warning you that if you try to run away, I'll catch you and it won't be pretty."

Slowly, Logan released the boy's arms. He backed up a couple of steps and waited for Jordan to turn toward him.

"Are you going to call the sheriff?"

"Not yet. I'd like to see if we can work this out ourselves."

Jordan picked up the headphones Logan had knocked to the ground and placed them around his neck, keeping his gaze firmly away from Logan.

"I'm sorry about your mom," Logan said finally.

Jordan's head shot up and his eyes blazed. "Olivia is the one who should be sorry. My dad says that if she'd been more of a woman, her husband wouldn't have needed to go after Mom."

"Have you heard from her since she left?"

"She's called a couple of times." Jordan's hands clenched into fists at his sides. "She's in Arizona. Told me she loves me and that I can visit her over the summer. My dad yells, then begs her to come back. I don't care if she ever comes back, and I'm not going to see her."

"I don't blame you," Logan said quietly. "But it's not fair to blame Olivia. She didn't force your mother to leave."

"But my dad—"

"I understand what your dad is saying. He's angry. This must be really hard on him."

"He sits on the couch in the dark every night. I can't even get him interested in any hockey games, and he loves hockey."

"He loves your mom, and he's hurting. I imagine you are, too."

"I don't care about her," Jordan said, his voice an

angry hiss. "It wasn't like she was a good cook or anything. I can heat up frozen dinners myself."

Logan felt a mix of sympathy and admiration for the kid. He remembered what it was like to put on a tough attitude to mask the real pain and how much trouble that could lead to. He pointed to the letters on the wall. "You're going to have to clean that up."

"I'll be late for school."

"Enough time this morning to write out one word but not much else?"

Jordan glared at him.

"Come back after school. Wear old clothes because you'll be repainting that wall."

"What if I don't show?"

"Crimson is a small town, buddy. It won't be hard to track you down." Logan picked up the can of spray paint and the flashlight. The room was beginning to brighten as morning dawned more fully. "I'm going to be working on renovations for this building, and I'll come looking for you if there's any vandalism while I'm here. But I'm going to need an extra hand for the small stuff. You interested in making some money?"

The kid's eyes widened. "You're going to give me a job after I did this?"

"Give me your dad's number and I'll run it by him. I'll have an answer by the afternoon. We all make mistakes." Logan smiled as he repeated Olivia's words from yesterday. "You get this chance on one condition. You need to leave Olivia alone. Your mom leaving wasn't her fault."

"Some people are saying—"

Logan cut off Jordan's words with a wave of his hand. "Some people are idiots. Don't be one."

"Fine," the kid said on a huff of breath.

Logan held out his hand. "Give me your headphones."

Jordan shook his head. "No way. These are Beats. Do you know how much they cost?"

"I do." Logan took a step forward. "You can have them back once the wall is clean."

Jordan muttered a few choice curse words under his breath but handed over the headphones. He picked up his backpack from the floor. "School lets out at three. I'll be here after that."

"See you then." Logan took a deep breath as he watched the kid disappear through the doorway. He'd come back to Crimson for his brother's wedding and now he had a job in town and a potential delinquent on his hands.

For someone who prided himself on keeping his personal connections to a minimum, today was a big departure. He wasn't sure what had possessed him to offer Jordan work, other than recognizing a boy who was carrying a lot of emotional baggage on his shoulders and who might need an outlet for some of that pent-up anger and frustration. Maybe if someone had given Logan a little help years ago, his life wouldn't have gone off track.

He certainly felt out of his comfort zone right now.

He took some measurements and made notes about the state of the progress before heading to the address Olivia had given him. He walked the few blocks to her house near the center of town, hoping the morning cold would clear his muddled head.

The house was situated on a block of renovated Victorian two-stories. It had a large front porch. The exterior had been painted a sage green with white trim and shutters framing each of the windows. As a kid, he'd walked these streets with his twin sister, imagining which of the homes they'd want to move to. Anything would have been an improvement over the dilapidated farmhouse outside of town they'd grown up in. His oldest brother, Jake, still owned the land, but the house had burned down in a fire a few years after their mother's death.

As he stepped onto the porch, the front door opened. Olivia smiled nervously and gestured him inside. "I saw you coming up the sidewalk," she explained quickly. "Not that I was watching or waiting. I happened to be near the window…watering a plant…and you were…well, come on in."

He smiled as color crept into her cheeks and felt the anxiety his memories produced slip away. She wore a cream-colored turtleneck sweater and slim pants that made her legs look a mile long. Her hair was pulled back again, and he realized he wanted to see it down around her shoulders. To know whether it was straight or held a bit of curl, if it all would feel as soft in his hands as the bit he'd fingered during their dance.

"Good morning," he said as she scooted aside to let him in. He took a strange satisfaction in the fact that she seemed as affected by him as he was by her. It wasn't the six-year age difference that made his awareness of Olivia so foreign. She was in a totally different league than him. Normally he'd respect that invisible barrier. But something about this woman made him want to forget all of the very rational reasons she was not for him. Because as much as his brain understood that, his body wasn't cooperating.

"Do you want coffee?" she asked as she led him through a formal living room filled with antique furniture and real art—the kind that looked like it cost a lot of money. A few spaces on the wall were noticeably blank, but he didn't comment as he followed her into the kitchen.

"I'd love a cup," he answered, taking in the modern appliances and warm butcher-block counters. "Nice space," he told her.

Her hand faltered as she reached up to take a mug from the cabinet. "Thank you. The kitchen is my favorite room in the house. It's the only place that doesn't feel stuffy to me." She flashed a tentative smile. "The garage apartment is nice, too. It was going to be my studio, but..."

"You're an artist?" He pulled out one of the stools and sat at the island's counter.

"A painter. Sort of. Not really." She shrugged. "I like to paint and studied art in college, but I haven't had much time for it lately."

"I took a ceramics class in high school. Before I got suspended for the second time."

The mug she held clattered to the floor but didn't break. He watched as she scooped it up, set it in the sink and took out another one. He shouldn't have brought up his misspent youth, but he'd needed to remind them both how different their lives were.

"Were you any good?"

"I didn't have a chance to find out," he told her. "They put a lot of the troubled kids with one of the art teachers. Kept us busy and out of the way of the students who gave a damn."

She turned, her gaze curious. "Why didn't you care?"

"I was angry, stupid and young. A bad combination. I managed to graduate, mainly because the school wanted to be rid of me."

She set the cup of coffee in front of him. "Milk or sugar?"

He shook his head.

"But things got better after you left Crimson?"

"After a while," he answered as he took a drink. "I grew up. Realized I didn't have to turn out the way most people expected me to. I had a choice not to fail, to prove them wrong. I made that choice."

She took the seat across the counter from him. "Maybe the problems you had when you were younger shaped you into a person determined to be better."

He actually laughed out loud. "I've never heard anyone suggest that."

"I have a lot of experience putting a good spin on bad situations," she answered with a small grin.

How was it that talk about his wild past seemed to melt away her nerves? He'd brought it up to keep her at arms' length, not as an ice breaker.

Her smile slowly faded. "I wasn't sure you'd come today. I figured maybe once you'd left town you wouldn't be back."

The thought had crossed his mind more than once in the past few days. He'd even interrupted Josh on his honeymoon to run Olivia's plan by Sara. He'd figured his new sister-in-law would have something to say about Logan returning to town and working so closely with her friend.

To his surprise Sara had loved the idea. She'd told Logan that Olivia needed someone on her side, and he'd be the perfect person to take over the renovations. Even Josh had seemed happy that Logan would be spending the next month and a half in Crimson.

Logan wasn't used to people being happy to have him around. He'd felt as though he had an itch he couldn't quite reach ever since he'd agreed to this plan. He didn't know how to make it go away, so he was doing his best to ignore it.

"I gave you my word," he answered.

She nodded as if that made perfect sense. He wanted to reach across the table and shake her. Didn't she see that he was not worth the trouble he was bound to cause? Maybe that was what he found so irresistible about Olivia Wilder. He couldn't remember the last time someone had believed the best about him, whether or not he deserved it.

"I have the plans and the proposed budget." She pushed a stack of papers toward him. "Not that I want to cut corners, but if there's any way to reduce expenses, that would be a big help."

"You know I'm cheap labor." He was only teasing but loved the blush that colored her cheeks once again.

"That's not what I meant. I'm going to put some of my own money into the project. At least until I can line up more outside funding. The new mayor has the best of intentions, but his plate is overly full at the moment. There's a chance the community center could get waylaid if there's something more critical that needs money from the town. I don't want the work delayed any more than it has been."

"Where did you get the money?"

"What?" She looked at him as though she didn't understand the question.

He studied her. "You said at the wedding that Craig had drained your bank account. I know the community center is important, but you need to take care of yourself first. You don't need to do anything foolish just to get money. Things will work themselves out, Olivia."

She busied herself with emptying her mug into the sink. "Easy for you to say. And it's none of your business where I got the money."

"That's true," he answered softly. "But remember I'm on your side in all this."

"I sold my wedding ring to a jeweler in Aspen." She

whirled around to face him. "We'll be divorced within the month. I don't have any use for it."

He held up his hands, palms facing her. "I'm not judging you."

"Besides which," she continued, absently rubbing two fingers across the empty space on her left hand, "it was my grandmother's diamond. My parents gave it to Craig before he proposed. He didn't even have to spend his own money on a ring. That's how ready they were to pawn me off on him." She stared at him, eyes blazing, her chest heaving. "I practically had a dowry attached to me, as if I was some Regency spinster. I was twenty-eight at our wedding, not exactly an old maid."

"I hope you got a lot for it."

Her mouth twisted. "Enough to make sure the renovations will continue."

"If you're sure that's how you want to use it. You don't owe anyone in Crimson because of what your husband did."

She shook her head. "I owe this town a lot. It's the first place that's felt like home to me."

"How long were you and Craig married?" he asked, coming to stand next to her.

"Five years." She took the mug from his hands, his skin tingling where she touched him. "I'm thirty-two. Way older than you."

"Six years," he clarified. "Not way older."

She took a step back but he followed. "I could have been your…babysitter."

He tipped his head back and laughed. "My brothers and I would have had you tied up in minutes."

"I'm tougher than I look," she whispered, turning away.

"I bet you are." He placed a hand on her arm and she

looked at him over her shoulder. "You're not an old maid, Olivia. Not by a long shot."

Her gray eyes darkened as she looked at him. Hope and doubt crashed behind them and he had to resist the urge to smooth the crease between her brows.

Instead he said, "I went by the site this morning to see where to start."

"Is it bad? Are we behind? Do you need to hire a crew?"

He glanced up at her. "I have someone working part-time for me, and I'll bring subcontractors in as needed. A lot of it can be done on my own. I brought my tools up from Telluride."

"You can keep them in the garage. I had an extra key made although most people in Crimson don't bother locking their doors at night. I'll show you the apartment."

He followed her out the back door and across the driveway. He noticed a small Subaru station wagon parked next to the house. "The SUV, too?"

Her pace didn't slow. "It was bigger than I needed. I traded it in."

Olivia Wilder was more resourceful than he'd expected. "You really are committed to this community center," he murmured more to himself than her.

She turned to face him as she stood on the first step leading up to the garage apartment. "Do you believe we can do this?"

She was above him on the step and he tipped up his face to meet her gaze. Her skin was creamy and smooth in the sunlight. A pale dusting of freckles spilled across her nose. "I believe you can accomplish whatever you set your mind to."

"We're a team." Her eyes searched his as she spoke.

He'd been part of a team once. His twin sister, Beth,

had been his best friend, confidant and protector, and he'd been the same for her. Since her death ten years ago, Logan hadn't allowed himself to get close to anyone. Now this slip of a woman wanted more from him than he was capable of giving.

He couldn't tell her that. He wanted Olivia to get what she wanted, to regain her self-confidence or maybe discover it for the first time. He'd been too young, selfish and stupid to help his sister when she'd needed it. But he could help Olivia. And perhaps in the process he'd be able to rid himself of a bit of the blackness that had consumed his soul since Beth's accident.

"We'll finish the work on your community center," he told her. "It will be great."

Her smile was so open and trusting, it made his heart beat faster. Which was strange because before today he hadn't been sure he still had a heart.

Later that afternoon, Olivia turned around in one of the side rooms of the community-center building. "This is going to be where we do the kids' programs because it's on the first floor and close to the bathrooms. Upstairs we'll have yoga classes and adult workshops. The big room in the back will be for speakers and community events."

"You've got it all worked out."

She flattened the building plans to the work table in front of her. "I've been dreaming about this for almost a year. Craig was elected mayor just months after we came to town. I started volunteering at the visitors' center soon after. It was clear that the town needed a place like this."

Logan studied the plans. "This town needed someone like you."

She glanced up at him. "Thank you for saying that. I'm not sure it's true, but I appreciate hearing it."

As she watched Logan study the plans, Olivia thought she'd never felt more alive than this day. As excited as she was about the renovations, she hadn't been comfortable at the building site while Jeremy and Craig had been running the show. The community center was her baby. The sense of responsibility and ownership it triggered gave her heart a lift.

"I have a couple design ideas," Logan said slowly, not taking his eyes off the plans. "Logistical things as far as water lines and how to position rooms for the most practical use and flow when people come in to the building."

She peered over his shoulder. "Great. You're the one with the construction experience. I want to hear everything you have to say."

"Just like that?" He turned to face her as one corner of his mouth lifted. He was so close she could feel his breath against her cheek. "Aren't you going to tell me how this is your project and you're the boss?"

She swallowed hard and leaned back. "This is *our* project," she corrected. "I want it to be the best it can. We're a team. I'm not the boss. I've never been in charge of anything."

"Have you ever wanted to be?"

She glanced up and was struck by the intensity of his gaze. Somehow she didn't think he was talking about the renovations any longer. "We're a team," she repeated after a moment.

He gave a short nod and straightened. Olivia watched him walk to the window. His shoulders rose and fell as if he was having trouble catching his breath. She knew the feeling and placed a steadying hand on her own chest. Suddenly she couldn't put together a coherent thought about plans, construction or anything that didn't involve Logan's hard body and Olivia as the boss.

Fantastic. She'd become a certified cougar in a matter of hours.

A door slammed at the front of the building and a minute later a boy slinked into the room. "I'm here," he said, his narrowed eyes focused on Logan. "Some guys are having an airsoft gun war at the park, but instead of having fun, I'm stuck as your slave for the afternoon."

Olivia saw a quick smile flash across Logan's face. "You should have thought of that before you bought the can of spray paint."

"Spray paint?" she asked softly, her mind a little fuzzy.

The boy whipped around, obviously unaware of her presence in the room until she'd spoken. She recognized him as Jordan Dempsey. They'd even met a couple of times at town events.

She thought of her conversation with Jeremy Dempsey in the hardware store. She knew the two of them had been just as devastated by Melissa and Craig's betrayal as she'd been. Maybe more so. While she hadn't expected Craig to desert her, she'd known he was a serial cheater and she'd no longer been in love with him. She wasn't sure if she ever had. But Jeremy and Melissa had seemed happy in their marriage, at least on the surface. Although Olivia certainly understood looks could be deceiving. She wasn't sure what had motivated Melissa to abandon her family, but that kind of rejection could hit a kid hard. Olivia knew that from personal experience, as well. She was a regular expert on rejection.

From the daggers Jordan was shooting in her direction, she could tell exactly where he placed the blame for his parents' breakup.

"What's she doing here?" His chin jutted out in defiance, but there was the tiniest tremble in his voice. It made her heart ache.

"Olivia is running this project," Logan said calmly. "You know that, Jordan. Don't pretend otherwise."

The preteen boy's bitter gaze never left her face. "I said I'd help you. Take out the garbage and whatever else you need. I never agreed to talk to the trash."

Before she could even register the insult, Logan had stalked forward and grabbed Jordan by the collar of his fleece jacket. The material bunched in Logan's clenched fist.

"P-put me—"

"Logan." Olivia took one small step forward. "You don't have to—"

"Apologize," Logan told the kid, giving him a sharp shake before releasing him.

Jordan bent forward, coughing melodramatically. "I'm not going to—"

"He doesn't have to," Olivia offered quickly, taken aback at Logan's immediate instinct to protect her.

Logan bent down, his voice quiet but firm as he spoke to Jordan. "She is not responsible for what your mother did. You have every right to be angry, but not with Olivia. You think making her the bad guy is going to help you feel better, but it won't. That's something you're going to need to figure out real quick or you'll be facing bigger trouble than vandalism charges. Trust me."

He smoothed a hand over the boy's back, the touch surprisingly gentle given the way he'd been holding him moments earlier. "Apologize to her. Now."

"I'm sorry," Jordan mumbled.

"Look her in the eye."

The unshed tears Olivia saw glistening in Jordan's

eyes broke her heart all over again. "I'm sorry I called you trash."

"You will treat Olivia Wilder with respect and not just while you're here with me."

Jordan looked at Logan and nodded.

"I'm going to have my eye on you while I'm in town." Logan reached down and picked up a bucket and scrub brush, handing them to Jordan. "I don't want to hear about any trouble involving you. Got it?"

The kid took the bucket and brush and nodded again.

"Good. You can start with the spray paint in the back room. After the wall is repainted, I need a few things from the hardware store. I'll give you cash with the list."

Olivia saw Jordan's eyes widen. "You trust me with money?"

"Until you give me a reason not to," Logan answered. "You're a good kid, Jordan. Don't let your anger make you forget that." He pointed toward the back of the building. "Now get going on that wall. If you want something, there's soda in the cooler by the wall and chips next to it."

"Thanks," Jordan mumbled in response, but he looked relaxed as he disappeared out the door to the hallway.

"I'm sorry." Logan turned to Olivia. "I should have told you about Jordan. I caught him decorating the wall this morning before school. Not the most flattering language."

"Begins with a B, rhymes with witch?" she guessed.

He flashed her a smile. "You don't want to say the word."

She shrugged in response. "I was never much for cursing. But I've heard that particular word enough to recognize it. What happened when you found Jordan?"

"I scared the hell out of him," Logan said with an answering shrug. "Then told him he was going to work here after school and in exchange I wouldn't call the cops. If you don't want him here, I'll make other arrangements."

"I don't mind. This whole situation is probably hardest on Jordan." She studied him for a moment then smiled. "Is he your *crew*?"

Logan nodded. "Until I need more."

"You're a nice guy."

His mouth dropped open. "What's that supposed to mean?"

Her smile widened. "Just what I said. You're nice. You want to do the right thing. Most people wouldn't have given that kid the time of day, let alone a second chance. Nice is underrated. It's a compliment, Logan. Say thank you."

"No."

His big shoulders shifted as if his shirt was suddenly too tight. She watched his fingers flex and knew she'd made him uncomfortable. The thought made her giggle a bit, since she'd been feeling slightly off balance all day. Misery loved company.

"Are you laughing at me?" A muscle in his jaw ticked.

"Near you," she corrected. Her skin felt delightfully warm all of sudden. Her whole body went tingly at the same time as a weight seemed to lift away from her heart.

She'd told Logan she trusted him and that was true. Her first instinct had been that he was someone she could count on. Watching him with Jordan had confirmed her belief. Despite his gruffness and clear intention to scare the kid straight, Logan wanted to help Jordan. Just like he'd agreed to help her.

She'd keep her attraction to him secret. He was still too young and too handsome to look at her as anything but a friend. But what Olivia needed more than anything in her life was a true friend. The knowledge that Logan could be one made her almost giddy.

She was jolted from her musings as his hands wrapped around her upper arms. She hadn't even realized he'd moved. But now he was holding her, almost lifting her off her feet the way he had Jordan. His voice held a sharp edge as he spoke. "Don't trust me and don't depend on me. I'll only hurt and disappoint you."

She met his fiery gaze with a measure of steel she hadn't realized she possessed. "Everyone I've ever cared about has hurt and disappointed me," she answered softly. "I'm not sure I'd know how to function any other way."

He sucked in a breath at her admission. She was shocked that she'd said the words out loud. He drew her so close that his lips almost grazed hers.

He wanted to kiss her.

She could see it in his eyes, feel the electricity in the air between them. Heaven help her, she wanted to be kissed by this man. No matter how wrong it was. Despite the differences in their ages, their lives. Every part of her wanted to feel his lips against hers.

She knew that kissing Logan would change her. She was a woman who was ready for that change.

Nothing could have prepared her for this moment but she reveled in the unknown, leaning in ever so slightly.

Chapter Four

Logan took a step back, wrenching himself away from Olivia. He had to force his hands to release her.

She stumbled forward before righting herself. Her fingers—those long, elegant fingers—pressed against her lips the way his mouth almost had a moment earlier. Her eyes were hazy with confusion and something else he couldn't name. The truth was he didn't want to understand it, because it might demolish his razor-thin willpower.

"Don't trust me," he said again, his tone unsteady. There was an undeniable tremor in his voice, but he was damn sure he'd remain in control of this situation. "Go." He pointed to the door. "You have to go now, Olivia." Yelling wasn't necessary. She understood how serious he was because she left without another word, grabbing her purse from the table and practically running for the front of the building.

He wanted Olivia Wilder but he couldn't have her. Didn't deserve her. Of that he had no doubt.

Wanting things beyond his reach was familiar territory for Logan. He had no issues with lowering his expectations of what he could have, what was his rightful due.

He had a life, despite the fact that for several years after his sister died he'd tried to squander it away. He'd been convinced he didn't deserve to live without Beth, couldn't stand the pain of her loss. But that had changed, and if he was destined to be part of this world, he'd long ago decided to earn his place in it.

That was the only reason he was here with Olivia, he reminded himself.

She was nothing like his sister. Somehow he still saw in her the woman Beth could have become if their father's abuse hadn't broken her spirit. He felt the overwhelming pull of potential that never came to pass being back in Crimson. He knew he was no one's hero, but Logan couldn't resist trying to help Olivia.

The only way he could truly help was by resisting his own immense need for her.

He concentrated on the renovation plans once more. When Jordan had finished repainting the wall, Logan sent him to the hardware store and then began nailing sheets of drywall to studs in the main room. Most of the electrical work and plumbing already had been completed, which meant Logan would only have to deal with a few additional subcontractors.

There were a couple people he could call for help who would put him in touch with the guys he needed to finish the job. He'd try to keep the subs working on the project to a minimum, both to save costs and to maintain a low profile. Of course, there was more to this project than he could handle on his own or with the help of a preteen boy in the afternoons. But he wasn't sure of the reception he'd receive from people in town. Many of the companies in Crimson were family-run operations. Thanks to the reputation he wasn't sure he'd ever live down, almost everyone would remember him.

Just as well he didn't dredge up the past. Despite his brother's recommendation, he couldn't imagine anyone else in Crimson would be too pleased to have him working on such a public project. This wasn't about him.

He had Jordan help him move drywall until they both were covered with a chalky film. Once the kid had started talking, he hadn't shut up, sharing stories about school, the town and his father as fast as he could breathe. Normally, Logan liked to work in silence, but today he was grateful to be distracted from his thoughts.

After sending Jordan home around supper time, he cleaned up his tools and installed a lock on the front door. He couldn't imagine Olivia had many other enemies in town outside Jordan Dempsey, but why take chances?

He pulled his truck into Olivia's driveway, his stomach turning over as he thought of how he'd spoken to her earlier. It wasn't her fault that he hadn't been with a woman in almost a year. That was the only explanation he could come up with for his reaction to her. So what if she smelled amazing, a combination of lavender and spice that made him dizzy with need? He longed to trail his fingers through her soft, mahogany hair. He could imagine kissing every inch of her pale, creamy skin until her whole body flushed like her cheeks did when she looked at him. This train of thought was getting him nowhere but damn uncomfortable.

He owed her an apology but needed a long, cold shower first.

Just as he climbed out of his truck, he noticed another

car, a bright yellow bug, parked next to the garage. The door opened and a girl, or young woman he supposed, hopped out. She looked him up and down, her gaze unabashedly appraising.

"And who," she said slowly, "might you be?"

Before he could answer, the back door of the house flew open. Olivia stepped onto the porch, her hair swept up in a messy ponytail, arms wrapped around her waist to ward off the chill. She wore an awful fuzzy pink cardigan that had clearly been around for more than a decade. She'd changed into black sweatpants and shoved her feet into enormous Sorel boots. To Logan, she'd never looked more appealing. That fact only served to convince him that he needed to get this renovation project finished as quickly as he could and get the hell out of Crimson and away from Olivia Wilder.

"Millie?" Olivia said, her voice a mixture of shock and disbelief.

The other woman raised a gloved hand. "Hey, sis."

A few moments passed before Olivia reached out a hand to the porch's wood railing to steady herself. She hadn't seen her half sister since their father's funeral three years ago. That had been the first time they'd actually met, although Olivia had known about Millie Spencer's existence since she was a girl.

"What are you doing here?" she asked, swallowing against the dryness in her throat.

Millie reached in the backseat of her tiny car and pulled out a duffel bag. "I'm driving back to Virginia from California. Thought I might stay with you for a couple of days. Catch up and all that." She turned to stare at Olivia, her whole body tense, as if she expected Olivia to refuse her.

Which would be the smart thing to do. Olivia and Millie didn't have any kind of a relationship and why would they start now? But Olivia wouldn't turn away her only sibling, despite her mixed feelings. Her gaze flicked to Logan, who stood silently watching the two of them. Olivia had been raised to keep her dirty laundry private. It was ingrained in her. She couldn't bring herself to do anything different.

"Come into the house," she told Millie. "We'll figure things out."

She noticed that Millie seemed to relax with the knowledge she wasn't going to be turned away. She took a step forward then pointed one finger at Logan. "What about him?"

"I'm staying up there." Logan indicated the apartment above the garage.

"Interesting," Millie answered.

Manners forced Olivia to take the few steps down the porch and across the driveway. "Logan, this is Millicent Spencer. She's…"

"Your sister?" Logan answered for her.

She couldn't meet his gaze as she nodded. "My half sister. Millie, this is Logan Travers. He's—"

"Hot?" Millie supplied with a sly grin. She turned to Logan. "Nice to meet you. I hope we get to know each other better during my stay. You can show me around town."

He gave Millie a slight, almost indulgent, smile. Even that made Olivia's stomach burn. "I'll leave that to your sister." Lifting his gaze to Olivia, his eyes grew serious. "I'm sorry about earlier."

She studied a spot behind his shoulder. "No problem. Misunderstanding. Have a good night." She turned toward the house, unable to stop the heat rising in her face. "Let's go, Millie."

As she started up the steps, Olivia looked over her shoulder. Millie still stood in the middle of the driveway, her eyes glancing between Olivia and Logan, who was unloading a toolbox from the back of his truck. Silently, Logan headed for the garage apartment. Olivia watched him open the door, then shut it behind him without looking at either of them again.

"Are you coming?" Olivia asked her sister.

Millie shifted her bag on her shoulder and followed Olivia. "If all the guys in Crimson look like that, I should have come for a visit a lot sooner."

Olivia counted to ten in her head as she walked into the kitchen, moving to stand on the other side of the island from her sister.

Glancing around, Millie whistled under her breath. "Nice place. Can't wait for the grand tour."

"What's going on with you, Millie?" Olivia asked, her head starting to pound from the events of the day.

"Where's Craig?"

"Gone."

"On a trip?"

"For good." Olivia rubbed her fingertips against her temples, trying to relieve some of the pressure there. "He left me. Took off with his secretary and all my money."

"I'm glad you got rid of him." Millie nodded, seeming unsurprised. "He made a pass at me at Dad's funeral."

Olivia took a step back, feeling as if she'd been slapped. "Why didn't you tell me?"

"We'd just met. Officially, anyway. I didn't want to draw any more attention to myself. I'm sure your mother wouldn't have appreciated it."

Her eyes drifting closed, Olivia thought about her

mother's reaction. Diana Jepson hadn't even known Millie had attended the funeral. She liked to pretend her husband hadn't been keeping a second family near Washington, DC, for the better part of their marriage. But Olivia had been obsessed with her father's mistress and daughter ever since she first realized they existed. It was sick, but she couldn't help herself.

When Millie had shown up at the visitation the night before the funeral service, Olivia had spotted her immediately. Craig had been uncharacteristically supportive, offering to keep Millie away from Diana. Now she knew why.

"So, is the new guy your rebound boy toy?" Millie gave a small shake of her tiny hips, then made a noise like a growl. "I didn't know you had it in you to consider becoming a cougar."

When Olivia's mouth dropped open, Millie laughed. "I'm joking! You're not *that* old."

"I didn't…he isn't…we're not." Olivia felt like growling herself. "I don't want to know what you mean by *that old.* Not that it's any of your business, but he's helping me renovate a building downtown. It's a community center I've been working on."

Millie's big brown eyes, the same color as their father's, rolled. "Of course you have. Saint Olivia. Picking up the pieces of her husband's tarnished reputation."

Olivia heard herself gasp. Millie barely knew her but she'd put her finger squarely on the situation. "Why are you here?"

"I need a place to stay for a bit. I'm between jobs."

"I thought you were going to college. Have you graduated? Are you teaching now?"

Millie's expression turned guarded. "I'm taking a break. At the funeral you said you wanted to get to know me. That if I ever needed anything..." Her voice trailed off and she picked up the duffel bag she'd set on the floor. "I guess you were just being polite. Those Jepson manners are a real burden."

You have no idea, Olivia thought.

"Sorry to have bothered you. Should I friend you on Facebook instead? Is that more the relationship you had in mind?"

Olivia heard the bitterness in Millie's voice. The funny thing was she *did* want to know her half sister better. The timing was awful, but that seemed to be the current story of her life. "Of course you can stay. For as long as you need. It's been a tough couple of months. I'm on edge. The company will be good for me. For both of us." She took a small step forward and then stopped, not sure what to do next.

"It's okay if we don't have our long-lost sister reunion now. No need to hug." Millie gave her a sad smile. "But thank you," she said softly. "I could use a time-out from the world."

Olivia put her arms around Millie's small shoulders. Millie was petite like her mother. Almost pixie size, but she practically vibrated with energy. That had been part of their appeal to Olivia's father. The fun he couldn't have with his own wife and older daughter. Olivia had stopped blaming Millie for their father's sins years ago. "*I* need a hug," she whispered and it felt right when Millie's arms wrapped around her shoulders.

After a moment they both pulled back. "I also need a bath," Olivia said. "It's been a long day. I'll show you the guest room first. After I'm finished we can have dinner."

She took Millie upstairs to the spare bedroom, then made her way to the master bath. One of the reasons she'd pushed so hard to buy this old house in town was the bathroom's claw-foot tub. In Olivia's opinion, there wasn't much a long, hot bath couldn't help fix. She watched the tub fill with water and bubbles, then lowered herself in, hoping to soak away the emotions that were rolling wildly back and forth in her mind.

She dunked her head under the water, a habit she'd had since childhood when she'd needed to drown out her parents' bitter arguments. A garbled noise made her sit up suddenly. Wiping bubbles from her eyes, she listened. There it was again. It sounded like a scream.

Logan heard the scream just as he cracked an egg into the mixing bowl. It sounded like a woman and came from the direction of Olivia's house.

Without wasting a second, he bounded out the door and down the steps, barely registering the driveway's blanket of new snow on his bare feet.

He burst into the kitchen to see Olivia's sister holding a long butcher knife in front of her. Blood dripped onto the wood floor from the gash at the tip of her index finger. The cut didn't look severe but her chest rose and fell in an unsteady rhythm, almost as if there was another injury he couldn't see. Her eyes met his, huge against her pale face.

"Blood," she whispered and he saw a shudder roll through her.

He took a step into the room but stopped in his tracks as Olivia ran in from the hallway. His mouth dropped open at the sight of her. Water dripped from the ends of her wet hair and little patches of bubbles clung to the strands where they framed her face, almost making a halo effect. She'd obviously just come from the bath and hadn't bothered to dry off before throwing on the thin white robe that covered her. Covered her without leaving anything to his imagination. The water had soaked through; the soft cotton of the robe clung to her every curve. It molded around her breasts under the now-transparent fabric.

His eyes flicked down, then back to Millie.

"You're hurt." Olivia dashed forward, grabbing a towel from the counter as she went. As she bent to her knees in front of her sister, the robe sculpted across her back. Logan practically groaned as he glanced to Millie's face. She still looked dazed but a wan smiled played around the corners of her mouth. Logan realized she knew exactly where his mind had gone.

"It's not bad," Millie whispered, leaning her head against the cabinet. "I just…blood…I'm not good with blood."

"Shh." Olivia wrapped her sister's finger in the towel. "We'll get you cleaned up in no time."

"You might want to get dressed first. Not that you look bad for a woman in her thirties." Millie made a motion toward Olivia with her uninjured hand. "I clearly interrupted your bath and…"

Olivia let out her own little shriek as she looked down at her robe. She scrambled to her feet, one hand covering her chest as the other grasped the sides of the robe tight together. Her eyes met Logan's. The blush he found so intriguing colored her neck and face.

Once again his equilibrium was thrown off balance. He felt a complete lack of control, willpower or the plain decency that should keep him from staring at her when she obviously felt so uncomfortable. He couldn't stop himself and his eyes raked over her body. His hand rose of its own volition as if he could pull her to him, right here in the middle of the kitchen with her sister as a witness.

No.

He jerked back, focused his attention on Mille. "You'll be fine," he told her and turned on his heel to stride out the door.

It slammed shut behind him. He pressed against the house's brick exterior. Fluffy white snowflakes landed on his face as he took several steadying breaths. He could practically hear them sizzle as they melted against his overheated skin. If he knew one thing for sure, it was that he needed to keep a safe distance from Olivia Wilder.

Which was his plan until a knock sounded on his door an hour later.

Olivia stood on the other side, this time dressed in the biggest, frumpiest sweatshirt he'd ever seen. It hid every one of her sweet curves, but that didn't matter. The memory of them was seared into Logan's brain.

She held up a bottle of wine. "I'm sorry."

"For what?" His voice sounded gruffer than he'd meant it to.

"That scene in the kitchen. Millie. This whole day?" She smiled but he saw her chin tremble.

His resolve crumbled in an instant.

He motioned her inside. "Would you like a glass?" he asked as he took the wine from her hands, careful not to touch her skin directly.

"I don't want to bother you. If you're about to go out or in the middle of something..."

"Reading a book."

"Reading?"

He raised his brows. "A book. You've heard of them? I'm partial to American history."

She covered her face with her hands. "Of course," she said through her fingers. "I'm sorry. I didn't think..."

"That someone like me would spend his free time in such literary pursuits?"

Her hands lowered. "Not at all. But you're handsome, single and if Millie's reaction was any indication, at no loss for female companionship. I thought you'd be out or with someone."

"I *am* with someone."

Her gaze shot around the small apartment. "I'm sorry," she said again and he wanted to smile at how adorable she looked.

"You, Olivia." He reached forward and tapped one finger on the tip of her nose. That tiny bit of contact he could handle. "I'm with you right now."

"Oh." She bit down on her lower lip and he stifled a groan.

"Sit down. I'll pour you a glass."

He took a wine opener from a drawer and got to work.

"What smells like cookies?" she asked as she slid into one of the chairs around the small kitchen table.

His back stiffened. "That would be…um…cookies. Oatmeal raisin to be exact." He glanced over his shoulder to see her reaction.

"I'll admit to being surprised that you bake," she said with a small smile. "I don't know a lot of manly man bakers."

"Manly man," he repeated. "That's funny." He poured the cabernet into a glass and put it in front of her. "I've baked since I was a kid. I was pretty sickly then, bad asthma, allergies, regular bronchitis. I missed a lot of school and couldn't be outside too much. My mom and I would bake to pass the time."

"It's hard to imagine you a sickly kid."

He wiggled his eyebrows. "I grew out of it."

He saw her swallow reflexively and smiled again. She made him smile more than he had in years. He put a plastic container on the table and opened the lid. "Try one. I like breads and cakes, too, but cookies are my favorite."

She hesitated, then picked out one of the cookies. "They're still warm." She examined the cookie for several seconds before taking a small bite. Her eyes widened. "They're really good. Amazing, actually."

Logan felt an unfamiliar swell of pride. "Thank you. I'm not sure they go well with wine."

"Everything goes well with wine," Olivia corrected him and took another bite, moaning softly.

Logan turned quickly to the refrigerator, took out a beer, then sat across from her. It was better if the lower half of his body was hidden at this moment.

He watched her eat the rest of the cookie, marveling again at the elegance of her long fingers.

"I really am sorry about earlier," she said after she finished. "Millie's my half sister. Although I've known about her for decades, we only met recently. Our relationship is so new it barely exists."

"You've known about her but never actually met? How is that possible?"

Olivia shrugged. "She was my dad's best- and worst-kept secret." She took another cookie from the container, her full attention focused on it. "My father was a US senator for many years. He and my mother married while he was in law school at Harvard. It was practically an arranged marriage. Her family had the money and connections he needed to start his political career." She broke off a small piece. "It's eerily similar to my story with Craig. I'm not sure my parents ever really loved each other."

After taking a bite, she picked up the wineglass, twirling the stem between her graceful fingers. "My mother didn't want to raise me in the capital, so when I started school we lived outside Saint Louis. My father came home sometimes, probably not as often as he could have. He had a mistress in DC and they had a daughter."

"Millie."

She nodded and sipped the wine. "She's seven years younger than me. I found out about her when I was twelve. I heard my parents arguing in his office. My dad stormed out and my mother ran to her bedroom. I slipped in and found a letter from Millie's mom. It was campaign season so my father was in Missouri with us. There were pictures in the envelope. Millie's baby picture and some candid shots of the three of them together. They looked so happy."

She put the wineglass down on the table with a clink. Logan noticed her fingers tremble. "My mom came down as I was reading. She took the letter, ripped it in half and told me never to speak of the whore or her bastard daughter again."

"I'm sorry."

She gave him a sad smile. "I couldn't stop, though. I found both their address and the name of the school where Millie went when she was old enough. For years I searched my father's office obsessively for more letters, any information I could find. Once the internet became the norm, that was one more way for me to keep tabs on them."

"Why were you so interested?"

"My parents stayed married because it was good for my father's career. We were the family on the holiday cards, the one he'd parade in front of voters. Millie and her mother were the people he loved."

She held up a hand when he would have protested. "It's true. I guess I always wanted to know why. What did he get from them that he couldn't from us? Why did he love Millie more than me?"

Logan ached at the pain in her voice. He knew what it was like to want a parent's love and approval so much but never got it. "Have you talked to Millie about any of this?"

She shook her head. "It's part of why I invited her to visit. Now that he's gone, I should probably let it go, but I can't. I want to know what it was like for her. What he was like with her." She gave a shaky laugh. "My mother would have a fit if she found out, but I have to find some way to make peace with this. I think I need to before I can really move forward."

He pushed the plastic container toward her and smiled when she took another cookie. "So why are you here talking to me?"

"I don't know," she admitted, drawing in a shaky breath. "It's hard to talk to Millie about the fact that our father loved her more. To admit that out loud. Apparently Craig didn't take every shred of my pride with him when he left."

She took another bite of cookie and met his gaze. "Plus I wanted to apologize for earlier." She waved the cookie in front of her like a shield. "I didn't realize how I looked. I heard the scream and—"

"You don't need to apologize."

"Well, I am. Trust me. It was totally embarrassing for both of us."

"I wasn't embarrassed," he said softly but she ignored him, standing and placing her wineglass on the counter next to the sink.

"Millie's your age. If you want to…take her out while she's here, I'm okay—"

"Stop." He stood and took her hand, lacing his fingers through hers, something he'd wanted to do again since their first dance. "There's nothing to be embarrassed about," he repeated. "You were thinking about your sister."

She didn't pull away but wouldn't meet his eyes. "You certainly bolted fast enough, maybe because you were going to be sick after seeing me like that? I know I'm not as young as…"

He tipped up her chin until her gaze lifted. "I don't want to take out Millie and I wasn't going to be sick." He gave a shaky laugh. "You're in your early thirties, Olivia. The prime of life. You're a beautiful woman. I had to leave before I pulled away that robe to really see you. Every inch of you."

Her mouth formed a perfect O and he tried not to groan. He traced his thumb along her jaw while his other hand cupped the back of her head, bringing her nearer. When he was so close that he could feel her breath, he whispered against her lips, "You need to know how much I want you. I shouldn't do anything about it. I hope to hell I'm strong enough to resist you after this. But you need to know."

Then he lowered his mouth to hers.

Chapter Five

Olivia wasn't an expert at kissing. Craig hadn't often touched her once they had married and she'd only been out with a couple of guys before him. But even if she'd been kissed a thousand times, she knew nothing could have prepared her for this.

Every single one of her senses delighted in this moment. Logan's lips felt unbearably soft against hers. He kissed her gently, reverently, as if he wanted to savor the taste and feel of her. He smelled like spice and man. The combination did funny things to her insides, making them swirl and tingle with a need she barely recognized.

A tremor passed through him, subtle but letting her know that she wasn't alone in her reaction to the kiss. That knowledge gave her the confidence to lean in when he would have pulled away. She lifted her arms around his shoulders and felt the corded muscles there bunch under her touch.

He stilled for an instant, as if she had surprised him.

She'd surprised herself. Olivia had never been the type to make any kind of move. She was far more the wait-and-see-what-happens type. Although she didn't know what this kiss meant, if it was a one-time aberration or something more—and good grief, she hoped it was more—she was going to make the most of it just in case.

As if reading her mind, Logan deepened the kiss, his tongue dipping into her mouth, dancing with hers as his hands moved down her back to cup her bottom. He pulled her tight to him, his arousal hard against her stomach. She almost fainted dead away. He wanted her. There was no mistaking the fact that he wanted her.

To be desired by a man like Logan, someone strong and powerful and...six years younger than she was.

She pulled away suddenly and grabbed hold of the counter for support. What had she been thinking? Logan had agreed to help her with the renovation. He'd let her dump her family problems on him like a real friend. But it couldn't be more than that. They both knew it. She couldn't bear to take this any further and have him disappointed. Somehow she knew being rejected by Logan would be a million times worse than her own husband's betrayal.

"I'm—" she began.

"Don't apologize," he said. His breathing was as uneven as hers.

"I took advantage of you," she countered.

He let out a harsh bark of laughter. "I kissed *you*, Olivia."

"Because you felt sorry for me."

"Because I wanted to kiss you." He pushed a hand through his blond hair, tousling it in a way that made her want to brush it back into place. Because at her core, Olivia liked things in their place, even if that place kept her lonely and afraid. She didn't think she had the guts to live life any other way.

"I'm still old enough to be your babysitter," she told him, hoping that would freak him out as much as it did her.

He only smiled. "You couldn't have handled me back then."

"I'm not sure I can handle you now," she said, immediately regretting the words as his expression turned guarded.

"That's not a news flash for either of us." He looked angry and something more, but Olivia didn't explain her comment. If he was mad at her, so be it. She could deal with that if it helped her keep a safe distance between them. Because she was afraid she might do something really stupid and fall for Logan Travers if she let herself get too close.

"I should go. Millie will be wondering what happened."

He nodded. "I'm meeting with the electrician tomorrow to talk about rewiring a few areas based on the revised plan. Do you want to be there?"

"I trust you," she said, taking a step toward the door.

"You should have learned tonight that's not a good idea."

"I trust you, Logan," she repeated. "It's me I'm worried about."

Before he could respond, she hurried out the door.

The next afternoon Olivia cleaned up the painting supplies from the art class she'd just taught at Meadowbrook, the local retirement community. For the past six months, she'd had about fifteen regular students and loved her weekly visits and the chance to share her love of painting with such an enthusiastic group.

She'd just cleaned off the last of the brushes when she heard a knock at the open door.

Natalie Holt stepped into the room, her gaze taking in the canvases drying on easels around the room. "What are you working on this month?" she asked, her brows furrowing as she studied several of the paintings.

"Light and shadow in nature," Olivia answered. She picked a new theme for each month.

"Why is it that everything Mr. Crantaw paints ends up looking like a woman's hoo-ha?"

Olivia smiled at her friend's observation. "He's got a one-track mind, as I'm sure you know."

Natalie returned her grin. "Are he and Mrs. Miller still on the outs?"

"He was working hard to make her jealous by complimenting Molly Jenner's artistic talent," Olivia said with a nod.

"Wiley old coot," Natalie muttered but laughed.

Natalie was everyone's favorite nurse at Meadowbrook. She was dedicated and caring but could handle even the grumpiest of old men with good humor. She'd been the one to encourage Olivia to start teaching at the retirement home after they'd been introduced by their mutual friend Sara.

Now all three women were good friends, and Olivia was grateful for the women who'd helped pull her out of the depression that had engulfed her after Craig left town.

Natalie pulled a granola bar out of her pocket and sat on the edge of the table. She often spent her lunch hour with Olivia on the days Olivia taught painting.

"How's it going with renovations? Has Logan started on the building?"

The brushes Olivia had been putting away clattered to the linoleum floor. "Fine. Great. He had some new ideas for the plans, and I've got funding sources lined up so..." She knelt to pick up the brushes.

"So what's the real story?"

Olivia glanced up to see Natalie watching her. A knowing smile played on her lips.

Olivia felt her face grow hot and she concentrated on grabbing the last brush, turning back to the utility sink without looking at Natalie.

"He's damn handsome," Natalie offered helpfully. "And single."

"And six years younger than me," Olivia countered. "Do I look like a cougar to you?"

Natalie laughed. "You're not old enough to be a cougar. A lynx maybe, but not a cougar."

"This isn't funny." Olivia whirled around. "He's out of my league and you know it. What would people say around town? Olivia Wilder can't even keep her husband interested, what makes her think she could satisfy a young hottie like Logan Travers? I'd be even more of a laughingstock than I already am."

Natalie popped off the table, her expression thoughtful. "I was sort of joking. Not that I think you couldn't get a guy like Logan, but I had no idea you'd *want* a guy like Logan. I've obviously struck a nerve."

"What does that mean, 'a guy like Logan?' Do you think I'm a snob? Is that what this is about?" Olivia hated how petty and defensive she sounded, but she couldn't make sense of all the emotions rolling around inside her since last night. For someone who craved order and control she was doing a really bad job of keeping it in her own life.

"Whoa," Natalie said, hands up. "Let's start over. Are you interested in Logan Travers?"

"He's working on the building."

"You know what I mean."

Olivia dropped the paint brushes into the sink and covered her face with her hands. "He kissed me. I kissed him. I'm not sure how it happened. Millie showed up and I came out in my robe and it was all so out of control." She pushed the heels of her palms into her eyes. "I like control, Natalie. You know I like control. I don't know what to do. First Craig left and I'm alone, I'm broke and I'm humiliated. Then I get another chance in Crimson and Logan is willing to help. But now I don't know how to handle him or anything. It's too much."

"Honey," Natalie whispered, using gentle fingers to pry Olivia's hands away from her eyes. "You like Logan."

"Heaven help me, I do." Olivia took comfort in her friend's touch. "Not just because of how he looks. He's a kind, decent person."

She shook her head as one of Olivia's brows quirked. "I know he has a bad reputation, but there's more to him. I know there is."

"Sit down." Natalie motioned to a chair then checked her watch. "I have a half hour until my break is over. That may be just enough time to explain how Logan got that reputation."

Olivia slid into a chair.

"Of the three brothers, I know Josh the best," Natalie told her. "Besides Logan, there's an older brother, Jake. They had a sister who died. Their dad was an alcoholic.

Until Josh returned to Crimson, none of them had lived in town for years."

"Sara told me that much before the wedding," Olivia said.

Natalie nodded. "I was a year behind Josh in school and a couple of grades older than Logan. Jake was away at college when the accident happened. The sister, Beth, was Logan's twin."

"How awful," Olivia murmured. "And especially for Logan."

"He and Beth were inseparable as kids," Natalie confirmed. "The two older boys were gone by the time the twins hit high school. Josh took off for the rodeo circuit straight out of high school." She took two plastic cups from the cabinet above the sink, filled them with water and sat down across from Olivia, pushing one of them toward her. "By that time their dad's drinking was out of hand and everyone knew it. The twins started running wild, Beth especially. I think she'd been daddy's little girl and was spared some of his drunken meanness. But once she got a bit older, she rebelled."

"It was a car accident, right?"

"Her boyfriend was behind the wheel drunk. He ran off the road and flipped the car into a ditch. He and Beth died on the scene. There was one other passenger, but that boy survived."

Olivia gasped. "I can't imagine the guilt he must have felt. Does he still live in town?"

Natalie had stopped speaking to take a drink and water sloshed over the side of the cup as she coughed wildly. "He left for college and never returned," she said when her breathing calmed. "Beth's death took a toll on each of her brothers, as well. Josh and Jake came back for the funeral but didn't stay long. After that, Logan got into worse trouble all the time. Things got bad and when they hit a breaking point, he left town."

"You're not going to give me any details?"

Natalie looked at her for a long moment and finally said, "I'm sorry, Olivia. It's not my story to tell."

Olivia pressed her lips together. "And he hasn't returned to town since then?"

Natalie shook her head. "This is the first time he's been back to Crimson since that time. It means something, Olivia, that he's here now. That he's stayed to help you. I'm guessing that you mean something."

"It isn't—"

"Don't be so quick to sell yourself short. You don't have to let the circumstances of your life define you. Yes, your husband was a lying, cheating jerk. And your family tree is a little mangled because of your father's poor judgment and the fact that your mom lacked the backbone to leave him." Natalie pointed a finger at Olivia. "You are not your mother. You have a chance to make a future for yourself. I'm not saying that Logan is going to be a part of it, but it's too early to rule that out. People change. From what you've said, he's one of them. If it feels right, why not give it a chance?"

Olivia wiped at her eyes as she smiled. "You might be right about me. But you know what I think?"

"What's that?"

"You're not your mother, either."

Natalie closed her eyes and sighed then rose from the table. "Oh, look at that. Lunch break's over."

Olivia stood and hugged her friend. "Thanks for talking me off the ledge just now."

"Any time." Natalie pulled back. "I hope you'll never have to return the favor."

"I'm here if you need it," Olivia reminded her.

"Dysfunction loves company," Natalie said with a laugh.

"You have a point." Olivia laughed then walked with Natalie out the door.

Chapter Six

The following week, Logan walked into the local hardware store, Ted's Building and Supply, which sat on the edge of Crimson. Ted's had been around as long as Logan could remember. He was happy to see that it hadn't been run out of business by any big-box stores, as had happened in many other small towns around the state.

Still, he'd avoided coming in until now, keeping busy with projects at the community center that didn't involve new materials. He told Olivia it was to give her time to re-establish her credit. The truth was he didn't relish an encounter with Ted Stephens, the store's long-time owner. Olivia hadn't questioned him, though, just apologized for the additional complication of dealing with her ex-husband's debts.

She was so pure in her desire to do the right thing that she was willing to stand up and take the fallout for a betrayal she held no blame in creating.

Every day Logan was amazed and humbled by her.

She kept moving forward no matter what. He knew she was making calls to potential funders and applying for grants to raise additional money for the community-center project.

She came by the building each day to talk about her progress and to see if he needed anything to help his work, as though keeping him happy was her priority. Her faith in him made him want to work harder just so he could enjoy the look on her face as her vision of the building took shape.

She continued to make an effort with Jordan Dempsey, and although she never pushed him, Logan noticed the kid was beginning to soften under her kindness. Monday morning she'd shown up with a portable refrigerator along with healthy drinks and snacks to stock it. She'd asked Logan for help moving it into the building but made him promise not to tell Jordan the food came from her.

Logan had wanted to kiss her again at that moment, which made it the same as most other moments they were together. He hadn't done it, of course. She was hurt and fragile, that much he knew. He was attracted to more than simply the way she felt in his arms. He liked talking to her, listening to her ideas and the way she made him feel as if he had something of value to add to the conversation. He wasn't going to let his lust mess up anything, no matter how much he wanted her.

It was a new experience, having someone believe he was better than he'd ever been given credit for. He might not deserve her faith in him, but he was smart enough to try to keep it for as long as he could.

With that thought in mind, he forced himself to approach the front desk of the store where Ted Stephens stood bent over a stack of invoices. Although Logan's legs felt like lead balloons and his mouth was coated with dry fear, he cleared his throat. The old man looked up, pulling off his reading glasses as his mouth gaped in recognition.

"Heard you were back in town," Stephens said without missing a beat.

"I'm working for Olivia Wilder on the community-center project."

"Nice lady," Stephens commented. "Lousy husband."

Logan nodded. "I have some things to pick up and a decent-sized order to place. Before I do either of those things, I wanted to talk to you. To apologize again and tell you that if you don't want me in your store, I don't blame you. I'll respect your decision and handle things however you see fit."

The man rubbed a wrinkled hand over his face. He'd been old when Logan was a teenager, but now he looked positively ancient, with deep lines furrowing his suntanned forehead and his gray hair turned shockingly white.

"You get along all right after you left town?"

Logan shrugged. "I managed."

"If you hadn't called 911 that night, Artie would have died."

"I didn't know Jim had a gun. That hadn't been part of the plan."

It had been a stupid plan to start with, capping off two years of idiot moves trying to numb the pain of his sister's death. The incident at Ted's occurred the summer after high school graduation when Logan had just turned eighteen. He'd been getting into more and more trouble, everything from drag racing on the county highway to underage drinking. When his buddies had suggested that they get a bunch of spray paint from Ted's and tag the high school, Logan had gone along with them even though he'd known it was wrong. Ted's nephew, Artie, had been working that Friday night. Artie was in his late-thirties, a doughy pushover of a man, a guy who wouldn't give them any trouble.

Except he'd refused to sell them the cans of spray paint, knowing full well how they'd planned to use them. Logan's best friend, Jim Thompson, had pulled out a gun and things had gone to hell in an instant. Artie'd been shot, then Jim grabbed the cash, yelling at the other boys to follow him out. But Logan hadn't been able to move, riveted by shock at the sight of blood spreading across Artie's white T-shirt. Instead of fleeing, he'd grabbed a towel from behind the counter and had tried to slow the bleeding as he'd called an ambulance. Jim had been arrested and Logan had left Crimson, finally terrified enough by the trajectory his life was on to change it.

"Have you seen Jim since then?"

Logan nodded. "A couple of years ago, after he got out." He ran a hand through his hair. "I tracked down Artie, too. He seems to be doing well down in Denver."

"Yep," was Ted's only response.

"I should have realized what was going to happen and stopped it before Artie got hurt. I'll always regret that night. I'm sorry, Ted. This community center means the world to Olivia and I'd like to work with you. But you probably don't want me darkening your door. Just say the word and—"

"You were an idiot," Ted interrupted. "But from what I hear, you've turned out all right. I know you had it rough growing up. All of you kids did. Everyone knew how your dad got when he drank and that your mom wasn't strong enough to stand up to him."

"She did her best," Logan argued. His mother hadn't

been perfect, but at least she'd loved him. That was more than he could say for his father.

"The town should have helped. Someone could have stepped in when things got bad."

"You weren't responsible for us."

"Someone should have been." He straightened the stack of paper and cleared his throat. "You've made amends for the past, Logan. I don't hold any bitterness for what happened. You're welcome here, son."

Logan felt emotion coil and then loosen inside him. "Thank you," he said gruffly. "I appreciate that more than you know."

Ted lifted the phone receiver and pushed a button. "Harry, to the front." His voice echoed over the store's intercom. "We have a customer who needs assistance with an order."

Logan smiled at the older man. "Thanks, Ted."

"Do good on the community center, son. This town deserves it, and I have a feeling Olivia Wilder needs a break."

"I'll do my best," Logan assured him.

The next few days passed quickly for Olivia. She kept busy working on funding for the community center and checking on progress in the building. She loved spending time there with Logan, watching the center come to life through his hard work. A sense of ownership and pride was beginning to bud inside her. She was no longer so embarrassed by her situation.

The fact that she was doing something in Crimson— something *for* Crimson—gave her the confidence to be a part of the town once more. She took baby steps, a visit to the local coffee shop and bakery she liked so much, an early-morning trip to the grocery store in town. Yes, she'd gotten some obvious pitying stares, but most people had either been kind in their sympathy or steered the conversation to topics other than her cheating spouse.

She began to think of the community center as hers. When she got word that a national foundation was considering her request for funding for a director's salary, hope bloomed that she could actually create the future she wanted.

She held tight to that feeling as it helped chase away the fear and uncertainty that niggled at the corners of her mind. She spent more and more time at the building site, despite her inexperience with anything construction. She'd set up her laptop in an out-of-the-way corner or talk to Logan as he worked. At first, she thought she might be bothering him but he seemed to like her company, asking her questions about her past and keeping the conversation going until hours had passed without her realizing it.

Today she wanted to help and needed to be busy. After several frustrating hours dissecting family history with Mille, she'd headed to the community center. Walking in the front room where Logan was working, she picked up a hammer.

"Show me what to do." She waved the tool in front of her.

He looked over his shoulder and smiled. "You're going to break your finger with that thing."

"I need to help."

"You do help. Without your tenacity and talent for funding, the place would be gutted for condos now."

"I need to do more. I want to be more."

His smile was so indulgent it made her want to grind her teeth. Whenever she'd wanted to try something new and different as a child, her mother had told her, "Don't attempt to be better than you are." Those words became almost a personal mantra Olivia had carried with her for years. But she was tired of living according to other people's labels for her.

She gazed around the empty room, then back at Logan. "Please."

"Have you ever painted?"

"Is that a trick question?"

He shook his head. "I don't mean a canvas. I'm talking about walls." He turned and rummaged through a cardboard box sitting against the far wall. "Most of the rooms will be sprayed since the construction is new, but there are a few areas in the front around the staircase that need a brush and roller." He pulled out a gallon paint can and bristle brush. "I was going to have Jordan work on it this week, but if you want to get started, I'll keep him busy upstairs."

Slowly, she lowered the hammer. "I'll do it."

He eyed her dark jeans and cashmere sweater. "I have an old T-shirt in my truck you can wear so your clothes don't get messy."

She tugged at the hem of her sweater, realizing her outfit didn't match her request. It felt a little like her life right now. She was reaching for things she wanted but wasn't quite sure that who she was fit with her new desires.

Especially as they pertained to Logan. She met his eyes, wondering if he was thinking the same thing.

"Thanks," was her only answer. *Fake it till you make it* could become her new words to live by.

He handed her the paint can and brush. "There's an opener in the box. I'll get the shirt and meet you in front."

She spent the next several hours working by herself. She managed to finish almost the entire section of wall around the staircase. In the process, only about half her front was covered in paint.

She listened to the sounds of Logan and Jordan working in other parts of the building, the whir of power tools and the sounds of muffled conversation drifting out to her. She didn't mind being by herself. Olivia had always been comfortable with silence, probably because there'd been so much of it in her house growing up.

Logan checked in on her occasionally, complimenting her progress at the same time he laughed at the mess she'd made. She didn't care, though. She lost herself in the rhythm of the work, ignoring the ache in her shoulders and back as she concentrated fully on her job.

It was the first time since Craig had left that she was able to completely block out her feelings of abandonment and the constant question of whether he would have stayed if she'd been different. Right now, with the paint brush in her hand, being different didn't matter. It was enough just to be.

"You don't have to finish the whole thing tonight."

Logan's voice behind her pulled her out of her thoughts. She glanced up, surprised to see the sun fading outside the windows. "What time is it?"

"Almost six."

She scrambled up, dropping the brush into the plastic tray. "I've been painting for over three hours?"

"You seemed happy enough so I didn't want to disturb you."

"I like the progress of it and being able to do something productive."

He nodded. "You were certainly productive," he said with a smile. "This job would have taken Jordan the better part of a week." One eyebrow lifted. "Keep this up and I may have to hire you on full-time. You'll give the professional guys a run for their money."

She grinned at the teasing compliment. "Is Jordan still here?"

"I sent him home an hour ago."

"Oh." Somehow knowing she'd been alone in the building with Logan as evening fell made her stomach do funny things. "I'm sorry if I kept you late."

"You apologize way too much," he answered and bent to retrieve the paint tray.

"Force of habit."

"We'll have to work on that." He traced one finger across her cheek. The light touch sent a shiver through her. "I'll clean up this stuff. You might want to wash in the bathroom before you go. You have paint…well…you should see for yourself."

Olivia felt her cheeks grow hot. "Good idea," she said, and turned for the back hall that led to the bathroom.

"You didn't tell me it was everywhere," she said to his back fifteen minutes later. It had taken her that long to scrub the white streaks of paint off her cheek, forehead and nose. She'd looked ridiculous and chided herself for reacting to Logan the way she had when he'd probably been laughing at what a disaster she was.

He wiped his hands on a towel as he put the clean paint brush next to the utility sink. "I liked your enthusiasm for the job even if your technique needs a little finesse."

"Maybe you should have been a politician," she pointed out, hoping he thought the color in her cheeks came from scrubbing off the paint and not as a reaction to his comment. "You certainly have a way with words."

"I'm fine with my simple life, thank you very much."

She envied that in him, his simple life. Even though she knew he'd gone through a lot to finally get there.

"Simple is underrated," she said and pulled his T-shirt over her head. "Thanks for the loan. I probably owe you another one for all the paint splatters."

She held out the shirt with one hand as she picked at a dry paint splatter on her jeans with the other. When he didn't take it from her or respond, Olivia glanced up.

Logan swallowed as she met his eyes. Their deep blue depths went dark as they lowered to her body. "Where's your sweater?"

"The layers got hot. I left it with my jacket by the front door." She looked down at the white camisole she'd worn under the sweater this morning, then back at Logan. He hadn't kissed her again since that first time and she'd begun to wonder if she'd imagined it. Despite her conversation with Natalie, Olivia wasn't the type to make a move on a man, nor did she want to compromise the friendship they had. She'd done her best to ignore her attraction to him. They talked and joked and Olivia tried to forget that he was the most beautiful man she'd ever laid eyes on. She paid no attention to the way her stomach fluttered every time his hand brushed against hers.

Looking at him now, she thought maybe she wasn't the only one who'd been denying unspoken feelings. The way his eyes raked over every inch of her at the same time that his body remained rigidly still made her think he was trying to resist her as much as she was him.

"Logan?" she said softly, unable to ask the question that burned in her mind. *Do you want me the way I want you?*

"Yes," was his reply and she thought it might be an answer to her unasked question as well as a response to his name.

Neither of them moved for several long moments until finally she blurted, "You haven't kissed me again." Now that just sounded pathetic. Blood rushed to her head and she shut her eyes, too embarrassed to look at him when he laughed or rolled his eyes or whatever a guy did when a woman made an idiot of herself.

No response came and after a few seconds, she couldn't stand the quiet. She opened her eyes to find him directly in front of her. She was actually staring at his chest where the fabric of the well-worn shirt opened above the button to reveal a sliver of skin covered with a smattering of hair. She didn't move her gaze from that spot, not to his broad shoulders or the sculpted muscles of his upper arms. She didn't even dare breathe, afraid that if her senses took in any more of him, she might do something really stupid like leap onto him, wrap herself around his gorgeous body and not let go.

She stood absolutely still.

Until he lifted her chin with one finger. Just that light touch had her knees practically melting. When she finally raised her gaze to look at him, he leaned in, brushing his mouth against hers in the lightest, sweetest, gentlest kiss she could have imagined. She swayed into him, because heaven help her, she could barely stand.

He didn't deepen the kiss, just continued to treasure her mouth with the barest of pressure. She didn't know what to do, where to go with this. It was nothing like the kiss he'd given her in his apartment but somehow the need it communicated undid her.

He pulled away and his hand fell to her shoulder, whether to steady her or himself she couldn't tell. "I want to kiss you," he whispered. Then he took a breath and said more firmly, "I shouldn't want it, but I do."

"I'm sor—"

"Don't," he said, taking a step back. "Don't apologize to me, Olivia. Not for what's between us." His hand raked through his hair. "Just know that I want to do a lot more than kiss you. But I won't."

"Why?" She couldn't stop the question.

He retreated several more steps. "Too many reasons to count. Because I'm only in Crimson until this job is done. Because you deserve more than I can give you." He paused and then added, "Because you're married."

Those three words hit her like a gust of winter wind. "I've filed the papers. You know that. It's only a matter of weeks before the divorce is finalized." Of the reasons he'd given her, the reference to her marriage stung the most, as if she was betraying her vows when she'd been the one left behind.

"You're moving on with your life," he said slowly. "I admire you for that. But not with me. It can't be with me."

Olivia felt tears prick behind her eyes. "Thank you for your honesty," she said through clenched teeth, determined not to cry in front of him. "It's good to know where things stand." She summoned every bit of backbone she had, plus all the years of being taught to hide her feelings in order to present a calm exterior in this moment.

Who would have thought she'd get something useful from her mother's browbeating after all? "I hope this doesn't affect the work on the community center or our... friendship." She kept her voice steady, even as that last word tore from her throat.

"Olivia," Logan said, his own voice thick.

She held up a hand. "I'm having dinner with Millie tonight. I'd better get going."

"I'm sorry."

She turned away, then stopped. "Don't apologize," she said over her shoulder. "The rules apply both ways. As long as you're honest, you don't have anything to be sorry for."

She walked out into the cold evening. The air smelled like snow. It was the first week of April but spring was at least a month off in the Rocky Mountains. She didn't bother to put on her sweater or coat despite the frigid temperature. Humiliation kept her skin warm even as hot tears spilled down her cheeks. She climbed into her car and made the short drive to her house.

It was true she had dinner plans with Millie. Despite the myriad of questions about their father and Millie's continual insistence that Olivia had been the lucky daughter, Olivia enjoyed spending time with her half sister. It was surprisingly comforting to talk about your family to someone who had at least a slight understanding of the people involved.

Millie had been hounding her for a girls' night out for the past few days, although Olivia had been clear about her intention to continue keeping a low profile in town. Baby steps and all. But maybe she'd give in tonight. There were a couple of decent bars in town and Olivia could use a break from her normal routine.

She took a deep breath and dried the last of her tears as she walked up the back steps into the kitchen. Millie stood to one side of the island, arms crossed over her chest, her gaze angry as Olivia walked in the door.

Millie wasn't alone.

Olivia's mother was seated at the kitchen table, looking cool, elegant and as angry as Olivia had ever seen her.

As if this day could get any worse.

"What is *she* doing here?" both women said at once, pointing at each other.

"Don't speak over me," Diana said on a hiss of breath.

"Don't tell me what to do," Millie spat back.

"Mom," Olivia said, holding up her hand to quiet Millie. "I didn't know you were coming to visit." She stepped forward, then bent and gave her mother a quick kiss on the cheek exactly as she'd been trained to do. A regular Pavlov's dog.

"I'm your mother," Diana replied. "I don't need an invitation. I'm *family*. Family is always welcome."

Her emphasis on the word *family* was clearly for Millie's benefit.

"Gotta go." Millie picked up a duffel bag from the floor and slung it over her shoulder. "Nice seeing you, sis." She flashed a glare at Diana. "Let me know when the Dragon Queen is gone."

"Wait." Olivia hurried to stand in front of Millie. "You're family, too." Diana let out a loud humph behind her. Olivia rolled her eyes. "You don't have to leave, Millie. I'm happy you're here. We're sisters. Really."

Millie blinked several times, then narrowed her eyes as Diana coughed loudly.

"Would you please be quiet, Mom?" Olivia said, keeping her eyes on Millie. "I mean it."

"It's okay," Millie said after a moment. "I have an interview for a job at a Montessori school in Denver anyway. I was going to tell you tonight and head out this weekend."

"You don't have to leave now."

"I do." She pointed past Olivia and made a gagging motion with her finger.

"I see you," Diana snapped.

Millie smiled. "I know." She gave Olivia a quick hug. "I'm going to stay with some friends in Denver for a while. I'll call you next week."

Olivia wanted to argue but her mother sighed dramatically and she realized it was too much to have her half sister and her mother in the house at the same time. She nodded. "Text me how things go with the interview."

Her sister agreed, then walked toward the door. Just before shutting it, she turned to Diana. "I can see why Dad needed my mom so badly. It would take a lot to defrost a man after he'd spent time with you."

Olivia shuddered at her mother's outraged gasp. Leave it to Millie to go out with a bang.

As soon as the door shut Diana stood. "I can't believe you'd let that little bas—"

Olivia held up a hand. "Don't say it, Mom. You know I love you, but what Dad did wasn't Millie's fault. She's my half sister. You may not understand it and you don't have to approve, but I want you to respect my decision to have a relationship with her. If that's why you're here then—"

"I'm here because of your husband."

Olivia stilled. She'd been so unnerved by seeing her mother and Millie in the same room, she'd totally forgotten about Craig. She hadn't told her mother that he'd run off, just glossed over the current goings-on in her life during their weekly chats. Her mother valued commitment to a marriage more than anything. Diana had given up her pride, her heart and much of her life to maintain the pretense of a happy marriage, and Olivia knew she'd expect just the same from her. She knew her mother must have discovered the truth from someone else.

"How did you find out?"

Diana waved her perfectly manicured fingers. "Word travels fast, Olivia. One of my tennis friends came to Aspen for spring break. She heard rumors and I confirmed them. Why didn't you tell me?"

"Because I didn't want to hear that it was my fault."

"Blame isn't important. I learned years ago that you'll only make yourself crazy that way. What I want to know is what you're doing to get him back?"

"Get him back?" Olivia almost choked on the words.

"Maybe you didn't hear the full story, Mom. He cheated on me and ran off with his assistant, draining our bank accounts in the process. It's not my job to get him back, and I wouldn't want him anyway." That much was true. Olivia might be uncertain about her future but there was no doubt she didn't want it to involve Craig.

"Of course you want him back. He's your husband." Her mother leaned in, as if divulging a great secret. "You took *vows*."

"Which he broke!" Olivia's voice rose and she paced back and forth across the kitchen, needing an outlet for the anger bubbling inside her. She was either going to walk it off or strangle her mother. "I'm not going to have this conversation, Mom. I'm not you. Even if I wanted to, Craig left and I doubt he's planning a big reunion with me. But more important, I don't want him." She stopped and faced Diana. "My divorce will be final within weeks."

Her mother's eyes flashed. "You can't get a divorce. How will that look?"

"Like I'm not going to roll over while Craig humiliates and deserts me?" Olivia shook her head. "I don't care how it looks. You made your choice with Daddy and I may not have agreed with it, but it was your decision. All I ask is that you show me the same respect. I'm getting a divorce and I want to stay in Crimson. I've gotten additional funding for the community-center project I told you about. I hired a new contractor and it's going to open. It makes me happy, Mom. Happier than I ever was with Craig. I hope you can honor that."

"You're different," her mother said softly.

Olivia gave her a small smile. "I don't know if that's a compliment, but I'm going to take it as one."

"Do you need money?"

The question was a surprise. Olivia shook her head and said, "I sold the Mercedes and Grandma's engagement ring."

Diana's mouth tightened into a thin line. She looked away for a moment, then back at Olivia. "That diamond was bad luck for the women in our family."

Olivia let out a breath. While her mother's admission wasn't exactly life changing, it was more than she'd expected. She was done fighting today. "I can heat up some soup," she offered. "And put together a salad for dinner?"

"That would be fine. I only want what's best for you, Olivia. I hope you realize that." Before she could answer, her mother disappeared down the hallway.

Chapter Seven

Once he finished cleaning up at the work site, Logan drove the few blocks to Olivia's house, pulling into the driveway just as dusk settled. He was tired after a long day of work and frustrated from how he'd left things with Olivia. Somehow he always got mixed up around her. Mainly between what he wanted and what he knew was right.

Lights were on in her house and just knowing she was so close put every part of his body on high alert. He needed to relax. A quiet night was definitely in order. He almost laughed at the irony of that. For years he'd gone looking for trouble when he'd wanted to unwind. Now the most rebellious thing he did was use specialty chips in the cookies he baked. As odd as it probably appeared to most people, the change suited him just fine.

Something caught the corner of his eye as he got out of the truck. He bent down to peer into the window of Millie Spencer's Volkswagen bug. She sat behind the wheel, her hands covering her face, shoulders slumped forward. Something was wrong. He glanced up at the house again but didn't see any sign of Olivia, although she'd mentioned having dinner plans with her sister.

Against his better judgment, Logan opened the passenger side door. "Everything okay?"

Millie jumped so high she practically hit her head on the car's roof. He saw her wipe at her face before turning to him. Tears. Great. His favorite thing.

"It's all rainbows and sunshine out here. Where's your tool belt, stud?"

He folded himself into the small front seat. He'd gotten used to the way Millie teased him. She might look like a teenager, but Olivia's sister could make a sexual innuendo out of the most innocent comment. He had the feeling her forward manner was all an act, but he went along with it.

"I'm not interested in nailing anything at the moment."

She smiled, which was a big improvement over crying. "If you're not going to use it the right way, all that hotness is wasted on you."

"I'll take that under advisement." He shifted in the seat. How did anyone over five feet tall get comfortable in such a tiny car? "Aren't you and Olivia having dinner together tonight?"

"I'm heading to Denver to meet up with some friends. The nightlife in Crimson is lame-o."

He leveled her with a look, knowing there was more to the story.

"Her mom arrived today. Olivia didn't know she was coming. Let me tell you, Diana Jepson doesn't have much use for her late husband's illegitimate daughter underfoot."

Logan grimaced. "I can't imagine Olivia asked you to leave."

"No, but she wouldn't turn away her mother, either. The three of us in the house would be far too hard." She shrugged. "It's time, anyway. I've got a job interview and I can't mooch off a sister I barely know forever."

"She likes having you here."

"She likes having you here, too." Millie's eyebrow rose as if challenging him to argue.

"Olivia is an amazing woman. Stronger than she knows." Logan said the words out loud but wasn't sure if they were for Millie's benefit or his.

"She's damn near perfect. Always has been. But it's a burden to her."

He turned toward her. "What do you mean?"

"It's tough being so unflappable and resilient and proper. Everybody wants to let loose sometimes. Even Saint Olivia. It's hard to find your true place in the world when you're so used to living according to what other people believe about you. I understand that." She poked him in the shoulder. "I'm guessing you can, too."

He didn't respond so she continued, "The trick for someone like her will be to find a person who she can be real with and still feel safe."

"I'm not safe."

"You care about her."

More than he would ever admit.

He opened the door, letting a blast of cold air into the car. "If you need anything, Millie, let me know. Good luck on that job interview."

Without waiting for a response, he got out and climbed the steps to his apartment. Not his, he reminded himself. This was Olivia's house, her garage, her life. He was just passing through. He didn't belong. He could be her friend, nothing more.

It was his feelings of friendship that kept him glancing out the window as the evening wore on, monitoring the lights in the house. He wasn't sure what he expected to see, but from what Olivia had told him about her mother, it seemed like it wouldn't be an easy night for her.

He should mind his own business. That had become second nature to him in the past few years. But he couldn't stop worrying about her. Twice he'd put on his boots, ready to knock on her door just to check if things were okay. *Stupid*, he told himself. He'd never met Diana, but could imagine that he was not the sort of man she'd want consorting with her daughter at a time like this.

He'd just put a tray of brownie batter in the oven when something propelled him to the window once more. His breath caught as he noticed Olivia standing in the middle of the driveway, halfway between the house and the garage. It had begun to snow, big heavy flakes that settled on her hair and shoulders. She wore a long parka and in the dim light that came from the house, he could see that her eyes were closed and her lips moving.

He opened the door. "Are you trying to catch pneumonia?" he called out, aware that he sounded like someone's grandma.

Her eyes snapped open and she glanced back over her shoulder before walking to the bottom of the stairs that led to the apartment. Her mouth was drawn in a tight line, her skin rosy from the air and snow.

She gazed up at him. "I didn't want to bother you."

"You're not." He gestured past him to the apartment. "Come inside, Olivia."

She didn't move for at least a minute, as if weighing something bigger than whether to walk up the few steps.

Finally she took the first step. Logan felt the pressure in his chest release.

He closed the door behind her and took her coat. She wore flannel pajamas with a tiny floral pattern across them. They were demure, cozy and sexy as hell. Her hair and face glimmered with wetness as the snowflakes melted from the heat in his apartment.

"I don't know what I'm doing here. I'm sor—" She stopped herself with a wry grin. "My mom went to bed early and I didn't want to be by myself in the house." Her fingers worked at one of the small buttons on the front of her pajama shirt.

He nodded. "I saw Millie as she was leaving."

Her eyes drifted shut. "She hadn't been here long, but we were finally starting to move past all the stuff with our father and get to know each other. I expected to have more time with her. Now she probably hates me."

"You're the least hate-able person I've ever met."

"Thank you," she said, looking at him again. "I actually do know why I'm here." She continued to worry the button as she spoke. "You make me feel okay about myself. Like I don't have to pretend to have it all together or work to meet anyone else's needs. Like it's enough just to be me."

She was so beautiful and vulnerable standing in front of him it almost brought him to his knees.

"You're more than enough," he said, his voice ragged with the emotion he tried to tamp down.

Her mouth curved into a small smile and some of the shadows lifted from her gaze.

I did that, Logan thought. He was prouder of this moment than anything else he'd done in his life.

But he didn't move. As much as he wanted to cross the room and sweep her into his arms, he stood where he was. She needed him to show her whatever tiny sliver of goodness he had left in his soul. She was desperate for a friend and if it killed him, he was going to be that for her.

She watched him for several more seconds, then turned her attention to the counter. "You're baking." Her smile widened.

"Brownies."

"From scratch?"

"You wound me, Olivia." He clamped one hand to his chest, grateful to lighten the mood. "Of course they're from scratch."

She giggled and came forward slowly. "I've never met anyone who made brownies from scratch. You'd better not let it get out that you've got..." She waved her hand up and down in front of him. "All that going on and you bake, too. The ladies of Crimson will be beating down your door."

"All that?"

"Don't pretend like you don't know what you look like."

"I look like a guy."

"A movie star kind of guy." She shook her head. "Your brothers have it, too. You three must have wreaked havoc on the girls in high school."

He shrugged. "They were older, but I guess I had some big footsteps to follow in when I discovered women." He folded his arms across his chest. "When I wasn't busy with all my juvenile delinquent fun."

"I'd love to hear more stories of your troublemaking days, especially since you're turning into such an honorable twenty-something Boy Scout."

"Boy Scout?" he interrupted.

One of her eyebrows lifted. "At least where I'm concerned." She motioned to the bowl sitting next to the sink.

"But now I'm more interested in the fact that there's leftover batter." She opened a drawer and pulled out a spoon, dragging it along the side of the bowl.

She was playing with him, he knew. Getting her revenge for the fact that he'd ended the kiss earlier. She knew he wanted her. How could she not realize how much he wanted her? Clearly her goal was to torture him, to drive him to the limit of his willpower and then right over the edge.

What she didn't know was that he'd already been teetering on the brink for weeks. Almost since the first moment he'd laid eyes on her.

As she lifted the spoon to her mouth he took it from her, his hand covering hers. He bent his head forward and licked her knuckle where a bit of batter had dripped, sucking the sweetness from her skin. He tossed the spoon in the sink and ran one finger along the rim of the bowl. His eyes never leaving hers, he brought his finger to her lips. Her tongue darted out, tasting the chocolate and then pulling his fingertip into her mouth. The warmth and wetness and slight suction were too much for him and he pulled away, wiping his hand on a dish towel.

"Why are you doing this?" he asked through clenched teeth. He held the towel so tight he thought it might rip in half.

"Because I don't care." She took a step closer to him. "It doesn't matter to me that you're only in Crimson for a few more weeks. Or that you think we don't fit or that I'm too old for you." She placed her hand on his. "Or that my divorce isn't final."

"You aren't too old, and I didn't say we wouldn't fit." He loosened his grip on the towel and entwined his fingers in hers, his thumb tracing small circles on the inside of her palm. "I said you deserve someone better. There's a big difference."

He heard her small sigh. "That's not your decision to make, Logan. A lot of things happen in life we don't deserve. My father choosing his second family over my mom and me, my husband cheating and then stealing all of my money. Your sister's death. But we *do* deserve some happiness now. To feel good and real and wanted. You make me feel that way. I don't care about any of the rest of it. I need to feel more than hollow again. Does that make sense?"

He continued to run his thumb across her soft skin. It did make sense, and it scared the hell out of him. He'd gotten so used to feeling hollow that it had become the norm. Normal and safe. He'd locked away his pain, in part so it wouldn't control him.

All of the stupid things he'd done in life had been a result of lashing out from emotional pain he couldn't manage. The truth was, he was afraid to let Olivia in because being with her might open a floodgate of feelings he couldn't control.

When he turned toward her, to the need and nervousness in her expression, all of his worry seemed to fade away. Maybe he couldn't be the man she deserved, but he could damn sure try to make her happy. To erase some of the pain she worked so hard to hide. If he could fill her empty places without letting down his own walls, that would be enough.

He wasn't sure if his logic made sense, but he had to come up with a reason why it was okay for him to kiss her right now. He couldn't stop himself from taking her in his arms and was sick of trying to fight his desire for her.

He cupped her face between his hands and lowered his mouth to hers, tasting a sweetness that went far beyond the lingering flavor of chocolate on her lips. She was sweet as sin to him, and Logan had never been good at resisting a chance to sin.

He nipped the corners of her mouth and trailed his lips down her jaw to the pale skin of her throat. Her head tipped back to give him better access, and he felt, more than heard, her soft moan as he licked his way down to the collar of her pajama top. He felt her sway against him and he lifted his head again, claiming her mouth as he picked her up in his arms.

Her hands laced through his hair and her legs wrapped around his hips. Her response drove him crazy with need. The apartment wasn't large and it took him only a few steps to reach the bedroom. He yanked back the covers and lowered her to the sheet. He reached for her top button, but her hand covered his.

"You first," she whispered even as a trail of pink swept across her face.

"Whatever you want," he told her and, grabbing his shirt by the collar, pulled it over his head.

He followed Olivia's widened gaze to the tattoo inked above his heart. "My sister's initials," he explained.

She nodded, then swallowed. "All *that*," she said, motioning to his body. "And all this." She pointed to herself. "It may not be a fit after all."

For several minutes, Logan watched her. His brows furrowed and Olivia wanted to groan. Leave it to her to throw a big wet blanket of insecurity over the most exciting moment of her life.

"What do you mean, fit?" he asked slowly. "You're not a...you and Craig did have sex, right?"

A nervous laugh burst from her throat and she clapped a hand over her mouth. "Of course we...well it wasn't often but…I'm not a…" She scooted back against the headboard and tried to explain. "It's just that you're young and you look the way you do." She bit down on her bottom lip as she took in the wide expanse of his chest once more. "And I'm only this…" She tucked her hair behind her ears. "I don't know what you're used to, but I'm not sure I can compete. At all."

He edged closer to her. "There is no competition. No comparison." His hand reached out to flick open one button. "I swear to you, just imagining this makes me forgot everything else in my life, Olivia. There is only you."

Another button opened and she looked down as more of her skin was exposed. "I'm not wearing a bra," she said.

His eyes went dark although he smiled. "That's helpful." He trailed one finger along her flesh, above and around her breast, circling the nipple until her breath caught. It produced a feeling like nothing she'd ever known and her whole body went hot.

He could do that to her with one finger. She was in big trouble.

"I don't usually wear one to bed," she mumbled, hoping she could retain a tiny bit of control if she kept talking. "Not that Craig took much notice, but it's just not comfortable."

"I sleep naked," he told her and her mouth went dry.

"Thanks for sharing. I think."

His grin turned wolfish. "You don't have to be nervous."

"Oh, but I do."

"Nothing's going to happen that you don't want." He opened the rest of her shirt and peeled it back from her shoulders, his gaze tracking all across her body.

The way he looked at her gave her courage. "I want

it all," she whispered and he captured her mouth again, tugging her flat onto the mattress as he balanced his elbows on either side of her. He kissed her until she forgot her insecurities, her past and any other doubt about herself. Her world was this moment, this tiny sliver of need, desire and so much more.

His head moved lower, and he took her breast in his mouth. She arched into him, unable to believe the mass of sensation swirling through every inch of her. He shifted, tugging at her pajama bottoms, pulling those and her underpants down off her legs, leaving her exposed in every sense of the word.

Before she could gather her wits enough to be embarrassed, his hands moved up her thighs. Her eyes flew open as his fingers found her center, then his mouth followed. This couldn't be happening...she didn't—

All thought was lost as his tongue followed, and she nearly came off the bed.

"Let go, Olivia." His breath was cool against the heat of her. "Right now. You can trust me."

She ignored the words "right now" and focused on "trust me." As he continued to touch her, she did let go, allowing herself to revel in his intimate caress. Within moments her body went up in flames and she cried out, finally understanding how much she'd been missing in life.

She was still trying to catch her breath as Logan shifted up until he was next to her. Her limbs felt heavy with satisfaction as he turned her on her side and pulled her back against him. His arm came around her, curling her in tight as his fingers traced a pattern on her belly.

"I love the feel of your skin," he murmured against her neck, dropping kisses along her shoulders.

She tried to keep her voice steady as she spoke. "I don't think we're finished. You didn't—"

He nipped gently at the back of her neck. "I wasn't kidding when I said you deserve better than me, Olivia. But I'm going to give you as much as I can. And that's more than a roll in the sheets to burn off energy from a fight with your mother."

She stilled, shocked at how true his words were. She'd wanted a release tonight. A break from the expectations her mother couldn't help but put on Olivia's shoulders. She hadn't even realized it until Logan said the words out loud.

He whispered against her ear, "And not until your divorce is final."

That made her temper flare and she struggled to free herself from his embrace. He only held her tighter. "When we're truly together and I make you mine, I want to know you're not thinking of him or that you're now the one cheating. I want you to be free."

"Oh." *Oh.*

Her mind couldn't seem to put together a coherent thought or even another syllable. Because Logan Travers understood her, perhaps better than she did herself. It might be true that she didn't love Craig, but she still felt the weight of her marriage. Until the divorce decree came, she wouldn't be completely free. And she wanted that as much as she wanted the community center to be a success. She wanted to revel in her freedom, to know that she was in charge of her own life and her future. Her mother hadn't understood that when Olivia had tried to explain it. But Logan did. Without her saying a word, he understood exactly what was in her heart.

The thought both exhilarated and terrified her.

"It will be soon," she said, more to herself than him.

She felt him smile into her hair. "It can't come soon enough. When it does, I'm going to take you on a real date."

"We don't have to go out," she protested, thinking about how the local gossips would have a field day thinking Olivia was making a play for a man like Logan.

"I want the whole damn town to see you on my arm." He smoothed her hair to the side and nuzzled the nape of her neck. "I'm going to ply you with food and drink, then bring you home and do every wicked thing I've been imagining for the past few weeks."

"Oh," she repeated.

"I should warn you," he said softly, "I have one hell of an imagination."

The sun shone bright against the windshield of his truck as Logan drove out to Crimson Ranch, the guest ranch Josh owned. He rolled down the window a crack, breathing in the fresh, cool mountain air.

Spring came to the Rockies in fits and spurts. A day such as this made him feel as if winter was loosening its hold on the mountains, but weather at this altitude could change in an instant. April could be one of the snowiest months of the year, the heavy wet storms that rolled in like a banshee melting away within days. Logan didn't bother much with weather forecasts, but he liked varying temperatures and the anticipation of what each morning would bring.

A sense of anticipation had settled on his shoulders since his evening with Olivia two nights ago. He knew it would be at least another week until her divorce was final, but already he couldn't wait for it. Which was what had led to this unexpected call on his brother. He'd been out to the ranch last night for dinner with his niece, Claire, and Sara's friend, April Sommers, who was watching the property and Claire while Josh and Sara were on their honeymoon. Claire had gotten a text from her father just before Logan left saying they'd be landing in Denver this morning.

Logan should have given Josh more time to settle in, especially after a red-eye flight, but he couldn't take the chance of Olivia talking to Sara before he spoke with his brother.

He took it slow down the long driveway and parked near the barn. If he knew his brother, Josh wouldn't waste any time getting back to his horses and the business of running the ranch. Josh's precision focus and dedication had led to his success as a champion bull rider before an injury ended his career and brought him back to Crimson.

Although Josh's black Ford truck was parked in front, he wasn't there or anywhere on the property that Logan could see. He walked the short distance to the main house and knocked on the door.

Sara answered, pulling him into a hug before he could speak. "Logan, it's good to see you. Claire said you helped her with her homework last night."

"I was happy to help. You look even lovelier after the honeymoon."

She smiled. "Marriage to your brother agrees with me." He followed her into the house, closing the door behind him. "It was hard for Josh to leave from the wedding after only getting a couple of days with you."

"Really?"

"She's exaggerating," Josh said, coming down the hall. "I couldn't wait to get her alone on a beach." He took Sara's hand and lifted it to his mouth for a small kiss. "But it's great you're still in Crimson. We're just finishing lunch. Do you want something to eat?"

Logan shook his head and followed them to the kitchen. He couldn't believe how much Josh had changed in such a short time. The brother Logan had known had always been coiled tight, tension radiating through him. Even as a kid, Josh had been wound like a top, always looking for a means of escape from their home. Now he looked relaxed and at ease. Logan wondered if the changes were all Sara's doing.

"Glass of iced tea?" she asked.

"Yes, thank you." He could use something stronger to make it through this conversation but would settle for whatever he could get.

"We have cookies, too." She pointed to a tin on the counter. "But I guess you know that. April says you made them." She smiled sweetly at Josh. "Your brother bakes. He's got skills. That's pretty impressive."

"I've got skills," Josh replied, with a comical leer in her direction. "Just not in the kitchen."

Logan nearly groaned at the teasing between the newlyweds. He wanted to dismiss his reaction, but something that felt a lot like longing uncurled in his chest, almost clogging his throat with it. He took a long drink of the tea Sara handed him.

"I forgot about your baking," Josh said, plucking up one of the cookies. "Logan was sick as a kid," he told Sara. "While the rest of us were going crazy all over town, he spent his time with our mom in the kitchen."

"I more than made up for it," Logan answered.

"You were always mom's favorite." Josh said the words without animosity, but they still grated.

"Only because I stuck to her like glue."

"I'm going to answer the emails that have been piling up," Sara interrupted. She placed her hand on Logan's arm. "We're happy you're here. Come out for dinner again now that we're back." She squeezed him softly. "Bring Olivia. I want to catch up with her."

"I didn't mean that like it sounded," Josh said when Sara left the room. "I'm glad Mom had you. She sure didn't know what to do with Jake and me. Beth, either, really."

"Dad couldn't stand it, though." Logan put his empty glass on the counter. "He hated having a wimpy kid underfoot. You and Jake were out of the house so much, but Beth spent a lot of her time trying to keep his attention off of me."

"It wasn't your fault," Josh said quietly.

Logan sucked in a breath. He'd wanted to talk about Olivia and his work in town, not rehash their horrible childhood. "I knew she was headed for trouble. She was drinking, partying and dating guys way too old and experienced for her."

"It still wasn't your fault."

"Or yours."

"It took a while, but I know that now." Josh shoved the cookie into his mouth. "Do you?"

"She was my twin. It's like a part of me, some vital piece, is missing. I don't think that will ever change."

"Has being back in Crimson helped or made it harder?"

Logan thought about the memories that continued to flood his mind and then of Olivia's sweet smile. "A bit of both. You know I was pretty messed up after she died. I said some awful things to you and Jake at the funeral."

"That was a long time ago," Josh answered.

Logan jerked his head in agreement. "I just need to know that you're okay with me sticking around now that you're back."

"Of course. Once we get settled, I'll come check out

the community center. Things haven't ramped up yet with our summer preparations. I could give you a hand with some of the work."

"That would be good." Logan rocked back on his heels. He'd never been one for small talk.

"What else?" Josh asked suspiciously. "There's something you're not telling me."

"How do you know?"

"We may not be close but we're family. Call it a Spidey sense."

Logan took a breath then said, "It's Olivia Wilder."

A small smile tugged at the corner of Josh's mouth. "Damn," he muttered. "There goes twenty bucks."

Logan stared at him.

"Sara was convinced things were brewing between you two. I didn't see it, but I should know better than to doubt my wife."

"Smart man," a voice yelled from somewhere in the house.

"Stop eavesdropping, woman," Josh called back. He grinned at Logan. "Nosy as all get out, but I love her."

Logan crossed his arms over his chest. "I don't even know why I'm telling you this. I guess someone needs to talk me out of it, to remind me why I'm not good enough for her."

Josh shook his head. "It won't be me." He cupped his hands around his mouth. "Sara, I know you're listening. Do you have anything to say to my brother?"

Silence.

"There's your answer." Josh smiled. "All good from this end."

"Are you crazy? You know the kind of person I am."

Josh just watched him.

"I'm not staying in Crimson after this job. I can't be here long-term. She's educated, classy and I'm—"

"Do you want some cheese with your whine?" Sara called from upstairs.

Logan threw up his hands. "Is she always like that?"

Josh laughed. "All of those nonissues you listed are between you and Olivia. I'm guessing the interest isn't one sided."

"The whole town knows I'm a screwup." Logan paced to the edge of the kitchen and back. "They wrote me off a long time ago."

"They wrote off the whole lot of us," Josh agreed. "Hasn't stopped me from moving on. Leave the past where it is, Logan. Where it belongs. I don't know what your future holds. It doesn't sound like you've got a much better clue. You can't be any worse than Craig Wilder was to her. Have some fun. Not everything has to be so serious."

"You're right. I know you're right." But Josh knew what it was like to have fun, to blow off some steam with a woman. It was different with Olivia. That had the warning bells clanging like crazy.

He stuck his head into the hallway. "I'm not going to hurt her," he shouted into the silence, then jumped when Sara gave him a little shove back into the kitchen.

"That's good, because I'll kill you if you do."

She said the word through a sugary-sweet smile, but somehow he didn't think she was kidding.

"She's serious," Josh confirmed his thoughts.

Logan pointed at his brother. "You're crazy."

"Crazy for me," Sara said and looped her arms around Josh's waist. Josh hugged her tight to him and placed a kiss on her blond hair.

Logan scrubbed his hand across his face. "I've got

to get back to the job site. The electrician is meeting me there."

"Thanks for stopping out," Sara said. "I'm glad we had this talk." Her smile was earnest, but Josh shook his head above her.

Logan let himself out of the farmhouse. Despite the oddness of that whole visit, his chest felt just a little bit lighter.

Chapter Eight

Olivia had breakfast with her mom before driving out to the retirement center. "I want you to meet Natalie and some of the people from my class."

Her mother smoothed a hand over her already perfectly groomed hair. "I still don't understand why you spend your time teaching painting classes for senior citizens. If you want to pursue your interest in art there are several prestigious artists' groups based out of Aspen." Her mother pulled a small notebook out of her purse. "I jotted down the websites if you'd like to have a look at them."

Olivia reached across the center console, plucked the notebook from her mother's hands and tossed it into the backseat. She ignored her mom's outraged gasp. "I don't want to be a patron of the arts, mother. I want to teach painting. I like it in Crimson."

"It's so…*quaint*." Diana said the word as if it hurt coming through her lips.

"It's a good town." Olivia resisted the urge to beat on the steering wheel with her hands. "Nice people."

"They certainly don't seem to blame you for Craig's indiscretions. I can't believe how many people approached you this morning to speak negatively about him."

That much was true. They'd gone for coffee and muffins at Life is Sweet, the local bakery situated a few blocks from the community center. Olivia didn't know Katie Garrity, the woman who ran the shop, very well. That hadn't stopped Katie from insisting that Olivia's coffee was on the house to celebrate Craig's departure from town. Several other patrons in the store had given her a reassuring pat on the back or murmured a few kind words after that.

Olivia had thought her mother might faint on the spot. Diana's number one life rule was keeping dirty laundry private. But Olivia found solace in knowing that she might be harder on herself than anyone else had reason to be.

Present company excepted, of course.

"You can't stay here," Diana continued. "You'll need to come back to Saint Louis and make a fresh start. We can play down your divorce and reinvent you."

"I don't need reinvention."

"I've already spoken to a friend who's on the board of the art museum. You can start as volunteer in their fundraising office and if something opens—"

"Mom, you're not listening to me. I like it in Crimson. I want to stay here."

"Don't be ridiculous. Craig was the mayor. Everyone knows you've been deserted and humiliated. Don't fool yourself into thinking that wasn't pity on those people's faces this morning. Pity is a terrible thing to live with."

Olivia felt her face flame with angry color. "It's better than living without my pride."

Her mother was silent for several long seconds, then murmured, "I don't understand you, Olivia. This isn't how you were raised."

Thank heaven for small favors.

"Mom, let's not talk about this anymore today. I'd like you to meet everyone at Meadowbrook. I want you to know a little bit more about my life. Can you just honor that?"

"What about the community center? Are we going to visit your new project, too?"

Olivia swallowed. "Sure. I'd...planned on it."

Out of the corner of her eye, she saw one of her mother's brows raise. "I saw the young man you have living above your garage today. The one working on the renovations."

"Logan Travers."

"He's very handsome."

Olivia remained silent.

"And young. Not at all your type."

"Because my type is a smooth-talking slimeball serial cheater like both my husband and my father were?"

Diana sucked in a breath. "Don't talk about your father that way."

Olivia swung the car into the retirement center's parking lot. "Forget it, Mom. Just give me this, okay?"

Her mother's lips thinned, but she nodded.

Olivia's anger dissipated over the course of the morning. It was both the bane and blessing of her existence that she couldn't hold a grudge. It kept her from wallowing in the pain she felt but sometimes made her a repeated target for more hurt.

At least in this place she felt comfortable. Most of the

residents in the wing where she taught were playing cards when they walked in. They were happy to put the game on hold to give Olivia's mother a tour and then insisted on showing her the hallway where the paintings they'd finished were displayed.

To Olivia's surprise, her mother seemed to relax as she spoke to the senior citizens. Olivia had always assumed that her mother's charity work was done more out a sense of duty than a real desire to help others, but Diana was clearly engaged by this group.

Sara Travers was having lunch with Natalie in the break room, and Diana was polite and cheerful as introductions were made. Obviously, her two friends met whatever arbitrary standards her mother had in her head. Meadowbrook's director offered to take Diana on a tour of the rest of the facility at that moment, leaving Olivia alone with the other women.

She let out a long breath as the door shut behind her mother.

"Guess I'm not the only one with Mommy Dearest issues," Sara said with a small smile.

"She heard about Craig," Olivia explained. "She flew out to lecture me on how I should save face and continue to let him walk all over me."

"Your mother must have made one hell of a political wife," Natalie commented with a snort.

"I have no intention of following in her footsteps." Olivia reached forward and snagged a baby carrot from Natalie's lunch.

"Logan came by the ranch yesterday," Sara said to no one in particular.

A bite of carrot lodged in the back of Olivia's throat, and she coughed wildly.

"Subtle as ever, Sara," Natalie said with a shake of

her head. She stood and clapped a hand on Olivia's back several times. "Okay?"

Olivia nodded and wiped at her eyes.

Sara gave her a glorious, movie-star smile. "Nice reaction. I think he wanted our blessing to date you."

"To date me?" Olivia sputtered out a laugh. "Guys like Logan don't date women like me."

Natalie tilted her head. "You're blushing. Something happened. What happened?" She took Olivia by the shoulders and shook her gently. "Let me live vicariously through you, Olivia. I'm desperate."

"Nothing happen—" Olivia closed her eyes. She'd always been a terrible liar. "We might go out. After my divorce is final."

"Why wait?" Natalie asked. "I'd jump a guy like Logan in a New York minute."

"They wait," Sara interrupted, "because he's a gentleman underneath all that bad boy hotness. *He* waits because Olivia's worth it."

"I don't know—"

"That's a good point," Natalie agreed, releasing Olivia.

"Stop talking about me as if I'm not here," Olivia muttered.

"We know you're here." Natalie gave her a playful swat on the shoulder. "Although if I was you I'd be camped out on the courthouse steps waiting for those divorce papers."

"Don't make it a big deal."

"You should have fun and let loose after what Craig did to you. Logan is the perfect guy for that."

Olivia thought Logan might be the perfect guy, period. But she didn't say that. "Can we not talk about this?"

"Only if you promise to divulge all the juicy details,"

Natalie said, wiggling her hips in a way that made Olivia blush.

"You really like him," Sara said, her mouth curving into a smile.

Olivia looked away. "Like you said, I want to let loose. Plus he's doing a great job on the community center. He's going back to Telluride when renovations are done. It would be stupid for me to *really* like him."

Her friends were silent for too long. She added, "My focus is the community center, which will be ready to open by next month. I had another grant come through yesterday. We've got enough money to run things through the summer. I'm starting to schedule classes and events. The mayor and a couple of town council members are coming to the building next week. I know some people are still nervous that I'm coordinating this after Craig deserted this town."

"You've done amazing work," Natalie told her.

"We need to throw a party. A grand opening celebration." Sara rose quickly from her chair. "A fund-raiser."

"What kind of fund-raiser?" Olivia asked.

"The kind where we raise a bunch of money and focus a ton of positive attention on you." Sara walked back and forth across the room, clearly in deep thought. "We could plan a reception to show off the place and everything you've done for it."

Olivia held up a hand. "I don't like being the center of attention."

Sara made a scoffing noise.

"You're the Hollywood actress," Olivia argued. "I'm a behind-the-scenes person."

"This is your time to shine." Sara held her arms out wide.

Olivia looked at Natalie and mouthed *help me.*

"You could make it about what the center has to offer," Natalie offered. "Call it an open house. Are you still planning on having a storefront with offerings from local artists?"

Olivia nodded.

"Perfect. Have some of them there to mingle with guests. The volunteers and teachers who will be working at the center can be a part of it, too." She turned to Sara. "April is going to be teaching yoga. She can be there."

"And you," Olivia said, pointing at Natalie. "You promised to let me sell your jewelry."

Natalie blinked several times, then busied herself cleaning up her lunch dishes. "Sure. Whatever. Although I'm not much of a draw."

"That's not true," Olivia argued. "Every time I wear a pair of your earrings someone compliments me on them." She brushed back a lock of hair to reveal the delicate gold loops Natalie had given her for her last birthday.

"It's true," Sara agreed. "Even in LA people stop me to ask about your designs. I think you could really make a go of it if you put yourself out there."

"I'm happy where I am." Natalie threw her leftovers in the trash can with a little more force than necessary. "Besides, this isn't about me." She gave Olivia a pointed look.

"Okay," Olivia said with a sigh. "It's for the community center. Let's do it."

Her mother walked back into the room at that moment. "Do what?"

"We're going to organize a fund-raiser for the opening of the community center," Sara told her. "To showcase all the work Olivia has done. How long are you planning on staying in town, Mrs. Jepson? We'd love to have you help plan it."

Olivia wasn't sure if she could take another month

with her mom in town. She held her breath, then released it as her mother said, "I need to get back to Saint Louis this weekend."

Her mother's gaze swung to Olivia. "Everyone here thinks very highly of you, Olivia." She sounded a bit stunned by the fact, and an awkward silence descended on the group.

"We love your daughter," Natalie said after a moment "She's one of us."

Diana pursed her lips but nodded. "I see that." She looked at Olivia. "Are you ready? I'd like to see this community center everyone speaks so highly of before I go." She glanced at Sara and Natalie. "It was lovely to meet you both."

They said their goodbyes as Natalie walked them to front door. Olivia and her mother headed to one end of the parking lot as Sara turned in the other direction.

"Say hi to Logan for me," Sara called over her shoulder. She winked in Olivia's direction.

"The contractor doing the renovations is Sara's new brother-in-law," she explained to her mother as they drove back toward town.

"The young man living with you?" Diana's voice was tight.

"In the apartment over the garage, Mom. We're not shacking up."

"Don't be vulgar, Olivia. Remember who you are and what's expected of you."

"As if I could forget." Olivia turned the radio on to avoid any more conversation.

Logan hadn't been at the job site when Olivia had taken her mother there. In fact, he seemed as eager to avoid a run-in with Diana as Olivia was.

Jordan Dempsey had been cleaning some things in one of the upstairs rooms, however, and had actually been polite to Olivia's mother without any prodding. When Diana excused herself to take a phone call, Olivia approached Jordan.

"I wanted to thank you again for all of your work around the community center."

"I didn't do it to help you."

"I know." Olivia kept her smile firmly in place. She refused to take Jordan's anger personally, even though it wore at her nerves. "Logan has enjoyed having you here."

The boy's chin jutted forward. "But he's going to leave. Like everyone leaves me."

Blown away by how similar her feelings were to Jordan's, she forced herself to count to ten in her head before speaking. "That's not true—"

"It is true!" Jordan threw his backpack to the ground. "I'm not stupid."

"I never said you were."

"My mom thought I was. I could tell something was wrong with her, that she was doing something bad even before she left. She was always texting or talking on her phone and then she'd tell me she needed to run to the store." He shook his head. "She never came back with any groceries. I wanted to tell my dad but I couldn't. He's so clueless. Maybe if I'd said something she wouldn't have left."

Her heart broke for this boy. "I understand why you feel that way, but it isn't your fault. The decision your mother and my ex-husband made was a bad one. They hurt a lot of people. I hope someday she can earn your forgiveness. But don't blame yourself for their mistakes."

Jordan blinked several times, his chin trembling. "Who else is there?" he shouted at her suddenly. "If she loved me so much, she would have never left. I wasn't enough for her. What if I'm never enough?"

Olivia felt the color drain from her face. She was so shocked by the boy's outburst, she couldn't form a reply. She almost crumpled to the floor and let his words, which mirrored her deepest fears, consume her.

Instead, she reached out and pulled the boy into a gentle hug. His shoulders stayed stiff for several moments before he deflated against her. "You're a good kid, Jordan. I bet your mom misses you every day. I would if you were my son."

He looked up at her, wiping his sleeve across his tear-streaked cheeks. "Do you think so?"

She nodded. "Adults make mistakes sometimes, even parents. But it's not your fault. She loves you no matter what."

He took a step back then leaned forward to give her another quick hug. "I'm sorry I've been a jerk to you."

"Apology accepted," she said with a smile.

Her mother called up from the first floor and Jordan turned back to his work. Olivia walked down the stairs feeling as if she'd finally gotten through to the boy. Perhaps Jordan would see that she wasn't the enemy. She knew a lot of that had to do with Logan's guidance. She explained Jordan's situation to her mother who'd been taken aback that Olivia would allow the reminder of Craig's mistress to be working under her nose.

But Olivia knew Jordan was just as much of a victim as she was. Jeremy Dempsey had even called to apologize for his outburst in the hardware store and to thank her for allowing Jordan to help at the community center. Jeremy also had asked if she'd heard from Craig and Melissa. She heard the longing in his voice along with the bitterness. It had renewed her anger at her husband, who'd not only turned her life upside down but also had destroyed another family. How could she have been such an idiot to actually marry someone like Craig in the first place?

Her heart went out to Jordan. She knew that even when his anger had been directed at her, she had been just an outlet for feelings that were difficult to manage. She often heard Logan speaking to him about responsibility and right versus wrong. Several times, she'd walked in on the two of them bent over Jordan's homework. Logan always played it off, saying that he'd skipped school so often that now he was trying to relearn some of the lessons. But she knew it was another way he was connecting with Jordan, making the boy feel special and cared for.

He'd done the same thing for her. Her mother left before the weekend. After that, Olivia and Logan fell into a pattern where she'd work on the business aspect of the community center most of the morning, then come to the building where he'd have some small job set up for her. Nothing technical or particularly taxing, but enough that she could feel as if she was contributing to the renovations.

They had dinner together almost every night, mostly simple meals in her kitchen. Craig had often worked late, or so she'd thought, although now she realized many of his late nights were probably spent with his mistress. But they hadn't shared many meals and Olivia forgot how much she enjoyed cooking. Logan didn't expect her to feed him, but he always complimented whatever she made and brought bread or dessert to round out the dinners. They talked and laughed and at some point each night, he'd pull her into his arms and kiss her senseless. His hands and mouth would roam her body as if he was attempting to memorize every inch of her.

He always stopped before either of them lost total

control. Olivia found herself resisting the urge to call her attorney for an update each morning. Then one day she walked out to the mailbox and her divorce decree had been delivered. There was no fanfare or big production, just a simple white envelope that pronounced her no longer married.

She didn't know whether to laugh or cry. Her marriage was officially over. She was free. Free to embrace her future with both hands. Free to become the woman she truly wanted to be.

Despite all her frustration over waiting to be with Logan, she suddenly knew it would be worth it. At the same time, a new kind of fear settled on her. She understood what it was like to have her hopes dashed.

All her fears and self-doubt came tumbling around her, but she pushed them aside. This was the new and improved Olivia, after all. Olivia 2.0. Olivia without the baggage of her no-good, cheating ex-husband.

Ex. Husband.

Her knees almost gave way and she leaned against the front door for support. She'd never expected to be facing her thirties divorced and alone. She'd done what she was supposed to for her entire life. First as a dutiful daughter and then as a good wife. All playing by the rules had gotten her were pain and disappointment.

Why not change her game?

With that thought spurring her forward, she straightened her shoulders and headed into the house. She didn't let herself think as she grabbed her keys from the counter. She made the twenty-minute drive to Aspen in silence, her heartbeat thrumming in her ears her only companion. She might be the new and improved Olivia, but she needed anonymity for this particular errand. It didn't take long for her to find the lingerie store—leave it to ritzy

Aspen to sell fancy undergarments in the mountains. Too embarrassed to try anything on, she let the saleswoman help her pick out a lacy bra and matching panties.

Olivia couldn't help the nervous laughter that bubbled from her throat as she drove back to Crimson, the noon sun high overhead. She parked in front of the community-center building and carried the tiny bag in with her.

Logan looked up from where he was measuring trim as Olivia walked in. He smiled as she came to stand in the doorway. Shifting her weight back and forth on the balls of her feet, she crumpled the small plastic bag in her hands.

"Hello, there," Logan said, wanting nothing more than to kiss her. But from the blush that covered her cheeks to the fact that she couldn't quite make eye contact with him, he could tell something was up. He gave her time to tell him what it was, although he had a pretty good idea.

"I have two things," she said shyly. "Two new things. Three really if you count—" She cut herself off and stared at the floor.

He took a step forward. "The first is?"

"I'm divorced. Officially." She scuffed the tip of one boot along the drywall dust on the floor. Logan could imagine that the blush that colored her cheeks covered her whole body. It made him crazy with want.

"We have a dinner reservation at The Church on the Hill. Eight o'clock."

She glanced up through her lashes. "How do you know?"

He shrugged. "I grew up with the manager. He's been holding a table for me every night for the past week. I wanted to be ready."

Her eyes widened and she thrust out the bag in front of her. "I bought lingerie. It's red and it matches."

Logan's mouth went dry. "You're trying to kill me," he whispered.

She drew back the bag. "I don't have to wear it."

He ate up the distance between them in three long strides. "In a good way." His fingers tipped up her chin until she met his gaze.

"Is there a good way to be killed?"

"When it involves you and red lingerie, hell yes." He kissed the corner of her mouth. "Are you going to show me?"

She clasped the bag tight to her chest. "I did this wrong. I'm supposed to surprise you later."

"I hate surprises," he assured her. "Let me see what I have to look forward to, Olivia."

She pulled back and opened the top of the bag. "I can't," she mumbled, then let out a shaky laugh. "I'm bad at this. If I can't even hold them up, I'll never be able to wear them."

He pressed his forehead against hers. "Oh, you'll wear them. You can't deny me the pleasure of peeling them off of you."

"I want tonight to be perfect," she told him.

"It will be." He'd gone over it in his head for what seemed like days, anticipating every moment, what he would say, how he'd look at her. If it was up to him, this was going to be the best night of Olivia's life. He forced his head back and looked in the bag. A tiny slip of red lace peeked out at him. His knees went weak, and he pressed the bag shut.

"Forget tonight. I think you should model this stuff right now."

"Here?" Olivia's voice was a high-pitched squeak.

He nuzzled his face against the side of her head, nipped at her earlobe. "I've decided I can't wait."

Someone cleared their throat behind where he and Olivia stood. "If this is a bad time, I can come back."

Logan's body immediately went stiff upon hearing the voice. It was gravelly, familiar and immediately ruined his day.

Chapter Nine

The evening was much different than Olivia had expected. The man who'd interrupted them at the community center turned out to be Jim Thompson, Logan's closest friend from high school. Jim had gone to prison for shooting a man. A man whose life Logan probably had saved by calling the police and having his best friend arrested.

She could feel the tension between the two of them, but Jim didn't seem to hold Logan responsible for his fate. He didn't need to when Logan clearly blamed himself for the events of that long-ago night, for letting his wild streak rule his life years ago, for not stopping Jim from pulling the trigger. Jim had committed the crime, but Logan still held on to a lot of guilt from that time.

Jim recently had been released from prison and had come through Crimson on his way to his sister's home on the Western Slope of Colorado near the Utah border.

Logan had seemed shocked to see his old friend, who'd tracked him down through people in Telluride.

Jim's arrival had changed their plans. Instead of a romantic dinner, the three of them had met Logan's friend Noah Conrad for burgers and beer at a bar in town. Olivia had met Noah several times while she was married to Craig and was grateful that Noah's affable nature brought some levity to their group.

Logan had been tense the whole night, barely making eye contact with her. At first she'd thought it was because he'd been left with as much pent-up sexual tension as she with no way to release it. Now, as she watched a trashy blonde she didn't recognize lean close to his ear while he lined up his shot at the bar's corner pool table, she couldn't help but wonder if his mind was simply elsewhere.

"Does it feel strange to be out after all that time?" Olivia asked Jim, hoping this conversation could distract her from how off track the night had gotten. She shifted uncomfortably on the bar stool where her lingerie-clad bottom had been sitting for the past hour. Were fancy underpants really worth this much fidgeting?

Jim Thompson looked at her over the rim of his glass. "I was sentenced eight years ago. The world feels a lot different now..."

She nodded. "Have you reunited with your family?"

"Reunited," he said slowly, as if testing the sound on his tongue, "is a funny word." He placed his glass of water on the table and studied her. "You ask a lot of questions, Ms. Wilder."

"I'm sorry," she said automatically. "Usually I mind my own business. But Logan doesn't talk much about his past or why he ultimately left Crimson."

"We were young and stupid back then." Jim gave her

a friendly smile. "No need to apologize. I don't think I should have come here, though," he added, his gaze following hers.

Noah gave Logan a quick high five after the shot, and the young woman said something that made Logan smile at her.

What had happened to make things go off track so quickly?

Sure, it was disappointing to have to wait a little while longer, but the change in him had been so immediate that she couldn't help but wonder if something else was going on.

She squeezed Jim's hand. "I'm sure Logan is happy to see you again."

"He was a better friend to me than I was to him back in the day. You know, he came to visit me every couple of months all these years. But I shouldn't expect that friendship to continue now that I'm out."

"Why wouldn't it?"

"Guys move on. I'm a reminder of the past he doesn't need." He shrugged. "That's why I was surprised he was here in Crimson. From what he told me, he had no plans to return anytime soon."

"He came for his brother's wedding."

Jim stared at her. "That's not why he's stayed."

At this moment, Olivia had no idea why Logan had stayed. His intentions toward her certainly had seemed to change in an instant. He'd barely said two words to her the entire night, other than to drop unsubtle hints about how Noah was single and available. He'd purposely sat her at the table next to his friend, and then pointed out all the things they had in common. Noah had handled it much better than Olivia, playfully flirting with her even though he seemed not to understand Logan's motivations any better than she did. She'd hardly touched her food and almost spat her beer across the table when, out of the blue, Logan had mentioned that Noah's favorite color was red.

The longer the night wore on, the surlier Logan had gotten, until Noah had pulled him out of his chair to play pool. The women had descended on the two handsome guys like a pack of starved vultures. The curvy blonde in particular had made a point of wrapping herself all around Logan, giggling into his face with regular frequency. She wore a low-cut tank top and short denim skirt that made Olivia wonder if she'd get frostbite on the way to her car at the end of the evening. It was obvious that if the woman had anything to say about it, Logan would be there to keep her warm.

He looked up at that moment and his gaze crashed into hers. She gave him a small smile, then cursed herself when his mouth tightened. Maybe being out tonight with women who knew what they were doing when it came to seducing a man had made him realize that she wasn't worth the trouble.

She watched him lean forward and say something to Noah, who returned to the table a few minutes later. "Do you want another?" Noah asked as he settled into the chair next to her.

She shook her head. It was clear that Logan had sent Noah to tend to her again. She'd never felt more like a charity case in her life. The humiliation of it was enough to spark her temper into a fast flame.

"You don't need to babysit me." She huffed out an annoyed breath.

"Is that what you think I'm doing?"

"I can't remember when I've had a more enjoyable evening," Jim offered.

"You've been in jail," she reminded him.

The corner of his mouth twitched. "Good point."

Noah's smile widened. "You don't seem like the type of woman who needs looking after, and it's definitely not a chore to talk to you."

"You forgot I'm the daughter of a politician and I was married to one. I can see the crap flying a mile away, and you two are neck-deep in it." She shot a glare at Jim. "Neither one of you needs to sit here, forced to keep me company because Logan's suddenly taken the notion to sow his wild oats with Crimson's finest." She slapped her palms against the table. "There's a group of guys hanging out at the bar. Maybe I'll just find my own entertainment for the evening."

She went to stand but both Noah and Jim clamped a hand on her arm.

"Not a good idea," Noah told her.

"And why is that?"

"Because I'm not much for bar fights anymore. Logan would go ballistic if any one of those guys looked in your direction."

She scoffed. "As if he has any right. You're saying it's okay for him to cozy up to the blonde who's shellacked herself to the front of him, but I can't even talk to another man?"

"You can talk to me."

"I don't want to talk to you," she said through clenched teeth, then remembered her manners. "No offense." She sank back into her chair. "You're a nice person and a good friend."

Noah made a face. "Nice?"

Olivia continued as if Noah hadn't spoken, "Logan doesn't owe me anything. I know I'm making a spectacle of myself." She plastered a smile on her face, hoping it looked more self-deprecating than watery. "You'd think I'd have gotten my fill of having men make me look like a fool by now."

"You're not the fool here tonight." Jim gave her a warm smile and stood, releasing Olivia's arm as he did. "But I see where this train is headed and I don't want be around when it hits the station. Olivia, I appreciate you letting me stay with Logan in the apartment for the night."

"Of course," she said, regaining a bit of her composure if not her pride. "It really was lovely to meet you."

He chuckled. "Ex-cons aren't called lovely very often." He smoothed a hand over his chest. "I think I like it." He picked up her hand and bent over it, dropping a gallant kiss on her knuckles.

Something crashed on the other side of the bar, making Olivia jump. But when she looked over, Logan's back was to her as helped the blonde bimbo line up a pool shot.

"The train is picking up speed," Jim murmured, releasing her hand and heading for the bar's exit.

Olivia began to pick the label off her beer bottle. "You really don't have to sit here with me," she said sullenly.

"I *really* want to," Noah answered.

"Thank you," she whispered and turned to look at him.

At that moment, the waitress sat a beer down in front of Olivia. "I didn't order—"

"It's from him," the waitress told her, hitching her thumb over her shoulder toward the group still standing at the bar.

"Oh," Olivia said on a tiny breath.

"Oh, no," Noah muttered next to her.

"No trouble," the waitress told Noah, pointing her finger at him.

"You're the one who delivered the drink."

She smiled at Olivia. "I knew Craig from when we were kids."

Olivia grabbed the bottle of beer and took a long swallow. Her throat burned.

"He was always a smooth talker but not much meat to him, if you know what I mean."

"I know exactly what you mean," Olivia said, rising slowly. "My divorce was final today."

She heard Noah groan.

"I'd say that's cause to celebrate."

"I thought I was going to but…" She trailed off and couldn't help that her gaze strayed to Logan. Who continued to ignore her, the big lug.

The waitress linked her arm in Olivia's. "Come over here, sweetheart. Let me introduce you to these fellows." She jabbed one finger on the table. "This fine lady deserves a bit of attention, Noah."

"What does it look like I'm doing, Amy?"

The waitress made a funny noise. "No trouble," she repeated and led Olivia away.

A half hour later, Logan smacked the cell phone out of Noah's hand. It skittered to the far end of the table.

"Dude. My eBay auction is ending in minutes. Do you mind?"

"Where the hell is she?"

Noah reached for his phone but Logan grabbed it and held it out of reach.

"She's at the bar," Noah said. "I'm keeping an eye on her."

Logan pointed to where several men stood laughing and talking in front of the bar. Olivia was nowhere to be seen. "She's gone. I asked you to look after her and she's *gone*, Noah."

"She can't be." Noah's gaze followed Logan's. "Damn," he mumbled.

Logan had half a mind to shove the cell phone where it would take a team of doctors to retrieve it. "You lost her."

Noah rose, standing nose to nose with Logan. "Back off, Travers. She wasn't mine to lose in the first place." He held out his hand and with more force than necessary, Logan shoved the phone into it.

"Was there a point to your little display at the pool table? I thought Josh was an idiot before he met Sara, but you give him some stiff competition. Why the hell am I sitting with your woman while you ignore her all night?"

"Because I…" Logan stopped before he revealed too much. Noah's affable, good—old boy charm masked a sharp perception. He knew he'd been a world-class jerk all night, but he'd been completely rattled when Jim had shown up. As much as he wanted to put his past behind him, he was afraid remnants of it would always find their way to the forefront. He couldn't stand to have Olivia tainted by who'd he'd been and what he might still be-come again. "She's not my woman. She needs to see who I really am, Noah."

"You're a half-wit who attracts bimbos. Point made. Nice work." His fingers punched in a few keys on the phone and he looked up again. "If that was the purpose of this entertaining evening, why do you care if she's gone?"

Logan closed his eyes to clear his mind but it didn't work. His whole head pounded from the frustration of trying to stay away from Olivia and the temptation she posed to his composure. He wasn't going to discuss this with Noah Conrad. "She's vulnerable right now. I don't want to see her get hurt. If she left with some jerk—"

"She left by herself." Amy, the waitress, came up from behind him. "Not for lack of trying by those guys."

Logan whirled around. "How long ago?"

"Why should I tell you?"

Logan gave her a look that would have had the surliest of bad boys running for cover. Amy only wrinkled her nose. "You look like your brother when you're ornery."

Noah tipped his head around to study Logan. "Josh?" he asked.

"I was thinking of Jake, but I guess they all have the same mad face. It's kind of cute."

Logan let out a low growl.

Amy gave a mock shiver. "Oh, that's very scary. I like it. Are you going to show me your teeth next?"

Logan took a step forward but Noah's hand flattened on his chest. "I thought you didn't want trouble," Noah said with a laugh. "When did she leave, Amy?"

The waitress flashed Noah a sweet smile before narrowing her eyes at Logan. "About five minutes ago. I wanted to buy her some time."

"Time's up," Logan said and turned for the door.

Noah pulled him back around. "Don't do anything stupid."

Logan stared straight ahead. "Define stupid."

Noah didn't speak for several seconds, then gave him a pat on the back. "Never mind. Right now, you look a lot like my definition of stupid."

"Thanks for the pep talk," Logan said and walked out into the cold.

Chapter Ten

It didn't take Logan long to catch up to her. Olivia's neighborhood was about a half mile from the center of town. By the time he'd left the bar, snow had started falling. Heavy flakes left a slippery coating on his truck's windshield as well as the roads.

Olivia was wearing boots, but not the kind made to trudge through snow. Hers were black, knee-high heels with dark denim tucked into them. He saw her moving slowly up the hill toward her house. She had on a light wool jacket and he knew the material of the black scoop-neck sweater she wore underneath was soft and thin. All night he'd been trying not to stare at her but he hadn't been able to help wondering if she was indeed wearing that red bra he'd caught a glimpse of earlier.

He pulled to a stop at the curb next to her, but she didn't look over at him. He beeped once, horrified when she whirled to face him and her feet came out from under her. He threw the truck into Park and jumped out, reaching the sidewalk just as she made it to her hands and knees.

"Don't come anywhere near me!" she yelled.

He felt like the biggest jerk on the planet. "Let me help you up."

"Don't touch me." Her voice was as sharp as a knife blade.

He watched helplessly as she struggled to her feet in the dim light from a nearby streetlamp. She dusted off her knees and smoothed her hands slowly along the front of her coat.

He saw her wince and took a step forward. "No," she said, holding up her hand. "I'm fine."

"At least I can drive you home."

"How did you tear yourself away from that rousing pool game anyway? I can't believe your barnacle would let you go so easily."

"My barnacle?"

She gave an irritated wave of her fingers. "The woman who's been stuck to you all night."

"I don't care about her."

"You obviously don't care about me, either."

"That's not—"

"Don't say it." She stalked toward him, slipping once. She righted herself as she stood in front of him, her eyes bright and spitting fire. "If you changed your mind, all you had to do was tell me, Logan. I wasted a lot of time and energy anticipating this night." A wry smile crossed her face. "And I've been dealing with the most uncomfortable wedgie in the world for hours." The smile vanished in an instant. "I'm a big girl. I'm used to rejection. Rejection I can handle." Her eyes focused on some spot over his shoulder. "But the public humiliation is getting old. I'm done with it."

"I didn't mean to humiliate you, Olivia. I promise."

"Right," she said on a ragged breath. "Dumping me off on your friends while you flirted with every woman in the place except me. That was a new low. Even Craig did his running around behind my back until the end. Everyone except me knew. I may have realized it somewhere deep inside. But at least I got to pretend."

The pain in her eyes sliced through him. He'd put that pain there, and he cursed himself over and over. "You don't understand."

"You're right. If you didn't want me, all you had to do—"

He grabbed her by the arms, ignoring her gasp of protest. "I do want you," he whispered, bending his head to look into her eyes. "I want you so badly it practically brings me to my knees every time I look at you."

He opened his gaze to her, let her see the intensity of his desire for her.

Her lips parted as her eyes clouded with confusion. "Then why?"

Releasing her, he turned away. "I thought I could ignore my past and it would go away. But today it landed on the doorstep in the form of Jim Thompson. How can I possibly risk tarnishing you with everything I've seen and done?"

"I'm not a fragile decoration, Logan. I can handle more than you think." She put a soft hand on his arm. "I liked meeting Jim. You obviously mean a lot to him."

With his back to her, he scrubbed his hands over his face. "He's been in jail, Olivia." Logan took three long steps away from her and then prowled back, stopping short before he allowed himself to get too close. "That's the sort of person I'm friends with. That's who I bring into your world."

He ran his hands through his hair, frustrated that she still looked at him with kindness. "I'm not good for you, Olivia. I've done bad things, would have done worse if I'd been given half a chance. I courted trouble and I almost consider myself lucky that damned night happened. It straightened me out when I needed it most. But it also changed me, or maybe Beth's death changed me. I don't know. But I can't be the man you need me to be."

"How do you know what I need?" There was a spark in her voice he hadn't expected.

He looked at her then, surprised to find her glaring at him, hands on hips. "I only meant—"

"I know what you meant. You think you know me. Everyone does. I'm the one who doesn't make trouble, who deals with whatever mess someone lays at my feet and then asks for more. I'm a doormat, just like my mother. I don't make waves. I smooth the rough edges for everyone else, right?"

He didn't answer but she was halfway to the truth. Olivia wasn't weak, but she'd done more than anyone else to smooth his own rough edges.

"There's more to me than that, Logan. I thought you saw it and that's why I wanted this. I don't want to be coddled or handled or pushed aside when things get messy. I don't need to be protected from you or by you. There's more to you than you think, too. That's why I wanted to be with you."

She paused and her mouth thinned. "Well, that and because any woman in her right mind and most who aren't would want to be with you. Mainly I want to feel again. To feel something for myself that doesn't have anything to do with my mother or my ex-husband or my responsibilities. I want it to be about *me*."

She jabbed the tip of one finger into her chest, as if

to convince them both. Logan felt his mouth drop open. She looked so beautiful and fiery standing in front of him, snow swirling around her head.

"You know what?" She looked over her shoulder and then back at him. "This night is about me. I'm divorced now. Single for the first time in years. I'm not going to slink home and wallow in some sorrow that I don't really feel. I'm glad to be rid of Craig. I'm better off without him."

Logan nodded slowly. "You are."

"Don't patronize me. I'm sick of people handling me with kid gloves. Somebody wants me, even if you don't. There's a guy in that bar who wants me. Someone who isn't too much of a coward to act on it." A brittle smile flashed across her face. "And I'm going to find him." She turned on her heel and walked away.

Oh, hell no.

Olivia made it half a dozen steps, propelled forward by righteous indignation, until her boot heel caught in a crack on the sidewalk. So much for a graceful exit. Her arms flailed as she went down, but before she hit the pavement, strong arms came around her middle. Logan hauled her up against his chest, pinning her tighter as she struggled.

"Don't lower yourself to going after some random hookup," he growled into her ear.

That's exactly what she wanted, an outlet for the tension and anger that coursed through her veins. "You're not the boss of me," she said, not caring how juvenile she sounded.

He held her close until she quieted. "You're better than this, Olivia." His voice was softer now, a gentle whisper against her skin.

She turned in his arms, assuming he'd push her away. His hold on her didn't loosen. She looked up into his face, surrounded by his strength and his smell. The anger she'd felt seconds earlier disappeared so quickly her legs almost gave out. "You are, too," she answered quietly. "You're a good man, Logan, in spite of the mistakes you've made."

She saw the pain in his gaze and something more, a tiny splinter of hope, as if he'd been waiting for someone to say these words to him all his life. For the moment she ignored her own hurt and chafed pride and spoke from her heart. "I believe in you. I believe you can make your life whatever you want it to be if you'd only give yourself a chance."

"All I want is the chance to earn it."

Her hands trailed slowly up his chest and neck until she cupped his face between her fingers. If he rejected her again now she might die on the spot, but she couldn't stop herself. "Then take it." She lifted onto her toes to press her lips to his mouth.

For several long seconds he didn't move. *This is it*, she thought. *This is where I test whether a person can actually die of embarrassment.* But when she went to pull back, his hand cradled her head, and he crushed his mouth to hers with a bone-stirring need that took her breath away.

He engulfed her with his heat, his desire. The kiss deepened until she couldn't tell where she began and he finished. He rained kisses along her jaw and neck, making her legs go weak when he traced his tongue over her racing pulse.

A moment later her feet left the ground as he scooped her into his arms.

"I can walk," she protested even as she snuggled deeper into his warmth.

"The next time you're on your back tonight," he said, his voice a whisper full of a promise, "is going to be when you're under me."

He opened the door to his truck and placed her gently on the seat, his finger pushing aside the hem of her sweater and delving down to trace the sliver of lace covering her hip. Her stomach turned to Jell-O at the touch. "You know that you don't have to buy any kind of special panties for me." His cool fingers traced along her burning skin. "I'd actually prefer if you wore nothing at all."

She swallowed hard as he closed the door and the truck's interior went dark. Her mind switched to overdrive as he got in and pulled onto the street. It was too bad, she thought, that he couldn't just have taken her there on the sidewalk. These minutes to think about what was coming were doing her nerves no good. She might want adventure but that didn't mean she wasn't scared out of her mind.

"Don't," he whispered, as if he could read her thoughts. "This is what you want."

She nodded dumbly, then shivered as her body finally registered the night's crisp chill.

Logan cursed under his breath and fiddled with the controls for the heat, turning the vents her way. They fishtailed slightly as he took a corner too quickly. The streets were empty but still she gripped the passenger door handle like a lifeline, needing to be grounded by something in this moment.

By the time they reached her house, Olivia was shaking in earnest. The melting snow had seeped through her coat and sweater. Her skin felt icy and her teeth chattered. She knew it was as much from nerves as the cold but she couldn't stop her reaction.

She'd only had one boyfriend before Craig and she

was a traditionalist at her core. When she'd married, she'd never again expected to have sex with a man other than her husband. Now here she was, single again and about to embark on an encounter with a man who was so different from her ex it was almost comical. She'd felt self-conscious enough with Craig, but what Logan might expect and how she was certain to fail him had her wanting to run.

Suddenly a part of her longed for her usual boring evening with cookies, milk and whatever chick flick she could find on TV. She was a lot less likely to make a fool of herself if she didn't try.

It took her a moment to open the door after Logan parked next to the garage. By the time she swung out her legs, he was waiting. She tried to shoo him away. "I can make it to the house," she muttered, then all but tripped out of the truck. He gathered her in his arms, taking her back steps two at a time.

"I'm fine," she said again, the words a little garbled, as her teeth were chattering so hard she could barely make a coherent sound.

"You're a human popsicle." He opened the door to the kitchen, kicked off his boots without putting her down and headed to the stairs. "Which one is yours?" he asked as he came to the top.

"All the way at the end." She buried her nose into the skin at the base of his throat.

She felt him twitch. "You really are freezing," he said on a heavy exhale.

"Y-yes," was her only answer because she didn't want to embarrass herself any more by trying to speak through her chattering teeth.

He set her on the edge of the bed and stripped off her coat before kneeling in front of her. He reached out and flipped on the small lamp on her nightstand. He sat back and unzipped one of her boots, his movements as quick and efficient as a mother might be when her child returned from playing in the snow. She closed her arms over her chest, moving her hands up and down to get the circulation going again.

"Lean back," he told her and she did so without thinking only to try to bolt up again as she felt his fingers on the button of her jeans. He placed a hand on her chest, gently pushed her down.

As he tugged her jeans down over her hips, she squeezed her eyes shut, then peeked out of one. Logan was on his feet, staring down at her, his blue eyes dark as his gaze raked over her body.

"I've changed my mind." His voice was a husky whisper. "The lingerie is worth it."

Olivia cracked open her other eye. "Worth riding up my back end all night?"

His mouth quirked. "It's a small price to pay."

She huffed out a small laugh. "Maybe for you."

"Only for me," he answered and bent forward to cover her mouth with his. As his hand trailed up her bare leg, she shivered again, more from his touch than the lingering cold.

He felt the movement and lifted off her, bringing her up into a sitting position and stripping her shirt over her head, tossing it aside with a jerk of his hand. Before she knew what was happening, he pulled back the comforter and shifted her so she was lying on the bed, head on the pillow. He turned her on her side and climbed in behind her, bringing the comforter back over both of them as he snuggled her into his chest.

She sighed as the warmth of his body began to seep into her. "What are you doing?" she asked after a moment.

"Reheating you." He pushed aside her hair and dropped tiny kisses from the edge of her shoulder to her neck.

"You're still dressed."

"You're still freezing."

It was true. Her body continued to tremble from the cold, but she also wanted...more. She squirmed in his arms; the fabric of his jeans chafed her bare skin. "I bet I'd warm up quicker if you didn't have so many clothes on." She grimaced as she said the words, hoping she didn't sound too desperate. Even though she felt pretty darn desperate at the moment.

"Stop making faces," he whispered against her ear. "There is nothing you can say that's going to shock me, Olivia. Anything you want, all you have to do is ask."

She turned her head to glance at him over her shoulder. "I want you naked."

The smile that lit up his face was both blinding and wolfish. "Your wish is my command."

He slipped out of the covers and she turned, drawing the comforter up to her chin. In one fluid movement, he shucked the shirt over his head. He reached into his pocket and pulled out a condom, tossing it on the nightstand before unbuttoning his pants and letting them drop to the floor, pulling his boxers down with them.

Olivia's mouth went dry as he straightened and she had to concentrate to take a breath. A body couldn't get any closer to perfection than Logan's. She'd known he was all ripped, powerful muscle, but seeing him—all of him—overwhelmed every one of her senses with desire she barely understood. His skin was smooth and taut with a dusting of golden hair across his chest and down his sculpted abs to... Her eyes flew back up to his face.

One side of his mouth curved into a smile. "I hope you're convinced that I want you."

She glanced down and then back up, covering her eyes with one hand. Yes, it was clear he wanted her, but she still couldn't quite understand why. He was perfectly built, way more experienced than she was despite their age difference and...

Oh, yeah, the age difference.

Olivia suddenly felt those six years as if they were a span of centuries.

As Logan climbed back into bed, she tried to scoot to the other side. He grabbed her waist and flipped her on top of him, their bodies touching from chest to toe. "Stay with me," he said, tapping one finger against her temple. "Don't overthink this, Olivia. Not now."

His hands slid down her bare skin and she felt his fingers flicking open her bra strap. "Tell me," he said as his calloused palms made circles on her back. "What next?"

She met his gaze and realized that he was holding his need in check for her, allowing her to take control. The gesture made her feel humble and powerful at the same time.

"Kiss me," she told him and he brought his lips to hers, plundering her mouth with a kiss that stole her breath.

Her desire took over, quieting the doubts in her mind. She wrapped her arms around his neck as he turned her onto her back. His mouth moved down to her throat, her breasts and belly and then lower. He found her center and she arched off the bed, moaning his name as pleasure overtook her. He took her to the brink, but before she crashed on to the other side, he grabbed the condom wrapper from the nightstand. She opened herself for him and he slid into her, her body stretching to accommodate him.

He whispered her name over and over, telling her she was beautiful and all the ways he planned on making her his.

They moved together, their bodies a perfect fit and Olivia felt the pressure build inside her. Just as it broke over, he claimed her mouth yet again and she cried her release into him as he did the same. His arms tightened around her and he tucked his face into the crook of her neck, kissing her softly as her body calmed.

"You're not cold anymore," he said after a few minutes. Although his words were teasing, she heard the tremble in his voice and knew that he'd been as affected by this moment as she was.

"I'm absolutely perfect," she whispered and he hugged her closer, shifting so that she fit against him, her head resting on his chest, their legs and arms entangled. She fell asleep feeling the steady rhythm of his heart against her cheek.

Chapter Eleven

When Olivia blinked awake hours later she was still warm and cozy, but it was the down comforter cocooned around her instead of Logan's arms. She sighed and told herself it was a sound of contentment, not disappointment over being left alone in the bed.

She'd had a mighty fine divorce celebration, better than she could have dreamed. Logan didn't owe her anything, certainly not a morning-after snuggle or whatever she wanted to call it.

Her hand splayed out across the sheets, smoothing the empty side of the bed. When she'd been married to Craig, Olivia had always tried to keep to her side, making herself small and still so as not to disturb him. The story of her life, trying not to bother the people around her.

A noise from the hallway caught her attention. As her head turned to the door, Logan walked through. A tiny chorus chimed a resounding *Hallelujah* in her head.

His brows furrowed as he came toward her. "You thought I'd gone."

"Maybe." She drew the covers up to her chin, embarrassed that she'd been ruminating on just that, and then feeling silly for being in bed still when he was up, dressed and showered, his hair wet on the ends.

He bent over her, one knee on the edge of the bed as he planted his hands on either side of her head. "I'm here," he whispered against her lips, his kiss minty, reminding her that she was still naked and rumpled and probably smelling a bit like the morning after.

She squirmed but he nuzzled his face against the base of her throat. "I love the way you smell," he said, with his uncanny ability to read her mind. "And I want nothing more than to strip down and join you, but..." His voice hummed against her skin.

"But..." she repeated, her brain feeling fuzzy.

"I have to drive down to Telluride this morning." He nipped at her skin where her pulse beat and she wriggled again. Lifting himself off the bed, he ran his hands through his hair and gave a quick laugh. "You have no idea what you do to me." His gaze swept over her and she tugged the covers down an inch, her ego rewarded by his soft groan.

"Sorry," she whispered.

He held up one finger. "No apologies."

Her smile widened. "Good, because I'm not really sorry."

He looked at her for several long moments, then said, "Come with me."

"To Telluride?"

"My meeting won't take long. It's just finalizing dates on a house project with one of the architects. We can spend the rest of the day together."

She had a few calls to make for the upcoming open house, but nothing she couldn't handle remotely. "I'd like that. If you're sure I won't be too much trouble."

He bent to kiss her long and thoroughly, a kiss that had her heating from the inside out. When he finally pulled away he rested his forehead on hers, his breath coming out in ragged puffs. "You're a lot of things to me, Olivia. Trouble would never be one of them."

Her toes curled at the emotion in his voice. "I just need to shower and get dressed."

He took a step back but didn't leave the room.

She sat up, taking the sheet with her and swung her legs off the bed. When he didn't move she shook her head. "I can't get up until you go."

"Why is that?"

She made a face "Because I'm naked."

"I know." His voice was a soft purr.

"It's broad daylight."

He wiggled his eyebrows.

Feeling heat rise to her face, she pointed to the door. "I'll be ready in twenty minutes.

He laughed but left, closing the door behind him.

Olivia hopped off the bed and raced to the bathroom. She barely recognized the woman who looked back at her from the mirror. Her dark hair was wild, tousled around her head. Her face still held a flush and there was a tiny love bite on the top of one breast. She should have been horrified but she felt delighted. She looked well-loved, satisfied, a little wild and…alive.

Alive in a way she'd never felt before.

She glanced around the bathroom at the morning light that slanted through the window. Everything looked clearer, in sharper focus. She could almost see the vibrations in the air. Logan hadn't abandoned her after their night together. That had to count for something.

She ignored the fact that a meeting in Telluride meant he'd be leaving after he finished the community-center renovations. She'd known that from the start, so there was no use pretending it was anything different.

From the way her heart kicked against her rib cage, it was clear she was going to hurt when he was gone. For now the pain felt like it might be a better alternative to the searing numbness she'd experienced for years.

She felt like Sleeping Beauty, waking after years of sleep. She laughed at how well the cliché, *It's the first day of the rest of your life,* fit her mood this morning.

If today was her first, she was going to do her best to make the most of it.

She showered quickly and then put on jeans, a fitted flannel shirt and snow boots. She picked up one of the bands she usually used to pull back her hair but let it drop to the sink. Instead, she finger-combed the wet strands, applied mascara and lip gloss, and hurried for the stairs.

She found Logan pouring a cup of coffee at the counter.

"I'm ready," she said, skidding to a stop next to him.

"You're quick." His gaze roamed from her head to her boots. "And very cute."

She didn't want to admit that she'd rushed so he wouldn't be tempted to leave without her. "I don't want you to be late."

"I grabbed muffins from the bakery."

Her stomach grumbled in response. She hadn't realized how hungry she was until he mentioned food.

"I got you pumpkin spice."

"That's my favorite," she said, glancing up at him.

"I asked the girl working the counter." He dropped

a quick kiss on the tip of her nose. "The sun's out this morning." He picked up the bag and handed her the coffee. "Most of the snow will have melted off the highway. It should be a nice drive."

She grabbed her down coat off the rack and followed him out the door. She looked toward the garage. "What about Jim?"

"He left earlier. Told me to say thank-you and he hopes to see you again."

"I really did enjoy meeting him, Logan, even if he did do something bad." She opened the door to the truck, then gasped as he turned her around and kissed her deeply.

"You're an amazing woman, Olivia."

She didn't know how to answer that, how to speak past the wellspring of emotion clogging her throat. She climbed into the truck silently, busying herself with the muffin and coffee instead.

The roads were almost empty as they started, although they began to see more cars as the morning wore on. The drive to Telluride was beautiful with the snow on the trees sparkling like diamonds in the daylight.

Olivia thought she'd never get tired of the beauty that surrounded her in Colorado. It was different than anything she'd known before she'd come here, but somehow it felt familiar and so much like home. They talked of everything and nothing, and the few hours from one mountain town to the other passed in the blink of an eye.

Logan pulled to a stop in front of a cute Victorian-style house near the center of town. As she climbed out of the truck, she shaded her eyes to look up at the ski mountain that loomed behind them. Although the temperature was warming quickly, snow still covered the peaks and a handful of skiers were making their way down the mountain.

"Do you ski?" Logan asked, meeting her on the sidewalk.

She shook her head. "Craig took me to Aspen Mountain the first winter we moved to Colorado. It was a total bust. He said I had no coordination and too much fear."

Logan draped an arm over her shoulder and bent to press a kiss to her hair. "If last night is any indication," he whispered teasingly, "you're both fearless and extremely coordinated."

"Oh, I was plenty scared."

He stopped, turned her to look at him, his concerned gaze raking over her face. "Of me?"

She bit down on her lower lip, wishing she hadn't said a word. But he clearly expected an answer so she said, "Of me. Of not being able to...well...be what you needed me to." She tried to step back but he laced his fingers through hers. "My husband was a serial cheater who left me for his mistress." She laughed, although it sounded more like a squeak. "It's not exactly a confidence booster."

His thumb rubbed against the soft flesh of her palm. She kept her stare firmly planted at the buttons of his corduroy jacket, unwilling to look up. All she could think was that he was trying to come up with something kind to let her down easy. It wasn't as if he hadn't...well, he'd seemed to enjoy last night. But sex was straightforward for a guy.

For her, being with Logan had been a revelation. Her body had responded to him in ways she hadn't expected. In her wildest dreams she couldn't have imagined how she'd want to touch him and be touched in return.

"Last night was better than anything I've ever known,"

he said softly. With one finger, he tipped up her chin. "You are amazing."

The words were so serious and sincere, she started giggling for real.

His eyes went wide. "Are you laughing at me?"

"You can't possibly mean that." She leaned up on tiptoe to kiss the corner of his mouth. "But I appreciate it anyway."

He combed his fingers through her hair, holding her tight when she would have moved away. "You have no idea what you make me feel," he said against her mouth, then kissed her so thoroughly, she felt the tingle in every cell. "But I have every intention of proving it to you later."

Logan ended the kiss and led her in to the house, which had been converted to offices. She still had a hard time believing his words. The thought that they were anywhere near the truth made her want to throw her fists in the air, Rocky style.

Olivia figured she'd live off the memory of last night for the rest of her life, so knowing he wanted to be with her again was deeply gratifying. She pushed aside her lingering doubts to focus on her present happiness.

Two hours later, Logan shifted uncomfortably in his chair at the small diner in downtown Telluride. He glanced back and forth between Olivia and Damien Cartman, the architect he'd worked with on most of his building projects here.

After the meeting about the current house Damien was designing, he'd insisted on taking Logan and Olivia to lunch. Damien was in his midfifties, wealthy, famous in the region for his mountain home designs and undisputedly brilliant. He also was as nosy as a bear in a campground.

It turned out he and Olivia had attended the same prestigious university back East, although during different decades. Logan listened to them reminisce about the campus, clearly feeling his lack of sophistication.

As if she sensed his mood, Olivia turned to him with a bright smile. "How did the two of you meet?"

Although Logan could imagine her thinking that someone sophisticated and worldly like Damien would never give him the time of day, her gaze held only curiosity. She was trying to make him feel as though he belonged in their little trio, much the way she had in Crimson, effortlessly easing him back into dealing with people from his past. But Logan didn't fit in and he had to make her see that.

"I sent him a fan letter." He took a long drink of iced tea, watching her from over the rim of his glass.

"Not the first I'd received," Damien offered at once. "But it made an impression."

Logan couldn't help but smile. Damien's ego was legendary, if well deserved.

"I got a book from the library about the mountain homes of Colorado," Logan explained to Olivia. "Damien's work was featured prominently. I was blown away by his designs and had a lot of time on my hands—"

Damien's broad chuckle cut him off. "The letter was part fan mail but a good portion of it gave me suggestions for how I might improve the construction principles."

Olivia's eyes widened. "You critiqued him?"

"Not my smartest move," Logan admitted.

"On the contrary, I was impressed." Damien bit off the end of one French fry. "I'd never received mail that pointed out things my team could do better. I was quite intrigued, so I flew down to Albuquerque to meet Logan."

"He offered me a job working with him," Logan finished. It had been the first time in Logan's life someone had reached out a helping hand to him. Damien became the lifeline that had changed the course of his life. By the time he'd met Damien, Logan had let go of most of the anger that had propelled him into trouble as a teenager. In its place was a gaping hole quickly filling with guilt and regret over the time he'd lost and the people in his life he'd failed. "I was desperate to get back to the mountains by that point, but couldn't stand the thought of going to Crimson. Instead, I came to Telluride and he helped me find a place to live, gave me a job. He changed my life."

Damien gave him a benevolent smile. "I may have the ego you say, but even I can't take that much credit. I saw the potential in you and you've more than lived up to it."

"That doesn't surprise me," Olivia said softly. "The community-center project in Crimson would have been dead in the water without Logan's expertise."

"It's only a simple remodel. Not that big of a deal," he argued.

Her eyes focused on him as she said, "It's a big deal to me."

Logan took another drink, unable to meet Olivia's searching gaze as his heart thundered in his chest. Maybe it had been a mistake to bring her with him today. Damien had expected a lot out of Logan these past few years—dedication, attention to detail, a backbreaking work ethic. Logan had been happy to channel his energy into Damien's projects in Telluride. He liked working with his hands, was gratified when a building or home took shape because of his efforts. But life in Telluride enabled him to keep his emotions in check in a way he couldn't in Crimson. Here there were no memories or sorrow to tug at him, no familiar scents or sounds that brought back images from childhood.

More important, there was no one like Olivia.

Logan could meet Damien's expectations, but wondered if the potential Olivia saw in him was more than he wanted to shoulder. He wasn't sure he could be the man she needed him to be, and it had nothing to do with his age.

He'd made peace with the past in his own way. He didn't do long term relationships and he never let anyone all the way in. Olivia deserved more than he was used to giving.

"Do you want to see pictures of some of the projects Logan's supervised?" Damien pulled an iPad out of his briefcase, looking at Logan with the kind of pride he'd never seen in the eyes of his own father.

"We need to get going," Logan answered at the same time Olivia said, "I'd love to."

He groaned but another layer of emotion unfurled deep inside him as Olivia viewed the photos, lavishing subtle praise at the same time she asked perceptive questions about design and materials. He could tell Damien was charmed by her and didn't blame the older man. She was kind and true in a way that captivated his heart.

How was it possible that she could adapt to any situation so quickly? Whether in a bar with an ex-con or discussing principles of line and symmetry with a renowned architect, nothing seemed to faze her. Did the ability to put all types of people at ease come from being a politician's daughter? No. Logan knew it was more than that. It was her genuine interest in people and her ability to accept them as they were. In fact, the only person he'd ever seen Olivia judge harshly was herself.

That was something he wanted to change. If he left her with nothing else, he could make her see that she was perfect just the way she was. Looking back, he understood that was the type of acceptance his sister had craved. Logan and his brothers, too. All they'd wanted in life was the one thing neither of their parents was able to give: the belief that they were good enough.

As the waitress cleared their plates, Olivia excused herself to go to the bathroom. Logan busied himself with his cell phone, checking emails and texts, but he felt Damien's perceptive gaze on him.

"She's the one," the older man said without preamble.

The cell phone flipped out of Logan's hands onto the floor. He bent to retrieve it, forcing himself to take a steadying breath.

"It's temporary," he said as he straightened. "That's all."

Damien just looked at him. "In the six years I've known you, there's never been a woman in your life."

Logan forced a laugh. "I've had plenty of women. Maybe you haven't been paying attention."

"*You* should pay attention," Damien corrected, pointing a finger at Logan. "I know you've chased your share of tail around this town. Not one of them has mattered until her. Olivia's different and you know it. She wouldn't be here if she wasn't."

"You don't know what you're talking about." Logan felt his pulse racing. He blinked several times as tiny sunbursts danced in front of his eyes.

"You deserve this, Logan. You deserve to be loved."

Logan's stomach rolled. A cold sweat broke out all over his body. "It isn't about love. She doesn't love me."

Damien was quiet for several seconds. "She could love you. She could help you."

He couldn't admit that she already had. "I'll be back in Telluride by the end of the month. Olivia will move on and so will I." His voice sounded hoarse and his throat was starting to close.

He hadn't had a panic attack since he'd left Crimson all those years ago. He'd spent the first weeks after Beth's accident trying not to go out of his mind wondering how he could have changed things. As twins they'd been a team, and he'd loved his sister more than anything. But it hadn't been enough. He'd failed her and since then he'd held everyone else in life at a safe distance. Until Olivia.

She was like the proverbial light at the end of the tunnel. But she wanted too much from him. He had no problem with working hard physically, paying his dues and building his reputation. The emotional stuff was a different story.

He lurched to his feet, braced his palms on the table. He had to get out of the restaurant before he imploded, needed to take a breath of cool mountain air and feel the calming heat of the sun on his face. "Tell her I'll be waiting outside." He bent toward Damien, keeping his expression tightly shuttered. "This *doesn't* mean a thing."

He turned then pulled in a harsh breath. Olivia stood directly behind him, a hand clutching her chest. All the color he loved so much had drained from her face.

He squeezed his eyes shut for a moment, then stalked past her, cursing himself with every terrible word he knew.

Chapter Twelve

Olivia stepped out of the small café, adjusted her sunglasses on the bridge of her nose. A few tourists milled about the sidewalk, but her eyes were drawn to Logan, who stood at the edge of the block.

She walked toward him slowly, her legs not quite working the way they were supposed to, her whole body heavy with sadness. She chided herself for that. He'd given her what she'd asked for, more than she'd expected. She'd had a night of passion to christen the start of her new life. She knew it shouldn't mean anything more than that. Yet...

It had.

She'd fallen for him. In love with him.

Her knees went weak and she pressed her palm to the restaurant's brick exterior to steady herself. The cold seeped into her hand. After a minute she smoothed her fingers over her cheeks, hoping to alleviate some of the heat she felt rising to her face.

She wasn't sure when it had happened, in the daily routine of working side by side with him at the community center or during the quiet nights of talking and laughing in her kitchen. She would have liked to convince herself it was only desire she felt, the afterglow of their intimacy.

Her heart wouldn't be deceived so easily. She loved Logan. It had happened in an instant and in a thousand little moments over the past weeks. He'd offered her friendship and a boost to the confidence and self-respect that almost had been wrung out of her.

She wanted so much more.

If Olivia was used to anything, it was yearning for things she couldn't have. Why should this be any different?

She took a deep breath and moved forward, coming to stand beside him. For the moment she pushed aside her own emotions so she could truly understand Logan's feelings.

"What a view," she said, following his gaze to the mountainside rising up at the edge of town. A frozen waterfall was suspended amidst the snow, high above the valley floor where the town was nestled.

"All I wanted after I left Crimson was to have the chance to live in the mountains again. It may sound strange, but I felt like I had to earn my place near them." His posture was rigid as he spoke but his voice was steady. "All that time growing up I took it for granted. I felt like I was trapped, but I had no idea how much I'd miss the solid presence of the Rockies at my back."

She smiled even though he wasn't looking at her. "They certainly put things into perspective. There's no questioning how small your life really is when you're standing in their shadow."

He shifted next to her. "I'm sorry you overheard my conversation with Damien."

Her gaze remained fixed on the place where the top of the mountain met the blue sky. "But not that you said what you did?"

"He pushes me too hard," Logan said, an emotion she didn't recognize making his words rough. "That's the way it's always been with him."

Out of the corner of her eye she saw his hand lift to her arm. "I'm sorry I hurt you."

"You were lying."

She felt him jerk away and angled her face to study him. She lifted her sunglasses to the top of her head, then reached out to pull off his as well. She wanted to look into his eyes. "I know what it feels like to mean nothing to someone, Logan."

She folded the glasses and tucked them into the front pocket of his jacket. Her fingers traced a small pattern along the fabric. "It was the same with both my father and Craig. They lived their lives however they wanted no matter the cost to anyone else. I was just a game piece to be played when it suited them and pushed aside when it didn't. There was never a thought given to my needs or what might make me happy. I was always in the background." She laughed a little. "Until I met you, I actually thought that was normal. Whether you'll admit it or not, you treat me like I matter. I'm learning that actions are more important than pretty words."

She could feel his breathing go shallow and harsh as she spoke. Emotion welled in her and she lifted her hand but he placed his over it. He brought her fingers to his lips, kissing each one of her knuckles with so much care it gave her goose bumps.

"I'm sorry," he said again. "You're right. I was lying.

I was scared and stupid and should have never said what I did. I don't know—"

She uncurled one finger and pressed it to his mouth. "You don't have to say anything. I'm not stupid. I know this isn't forever. But I'm okay with whatever you can give me."

The wind kicked up, blowing her hair into her face. With his free hand, he tucked a loose strand behind her ear, then cupped her neck and massaged the knotted muscles there. She wanted to melt against him. It was important that he knew exactly how she felt about him. "I want you to understand that it's enough. That you're enough."

She would have continued, explaining that he didn't owe her anything. Knowing that as much as she might want more, she'd never ask him for it.

Instead he captured her mouth with his, his kiss telling her everything she needed to know about his feelings for her. She swayed against him when he pulled back, wondering that her legs could hold her at all.

"I want to show you something," he said, bringing her to where his truck was parked up the street.

She'd meant what she said. She'd take him, as much of him as he'd let her have. She'd deal with the consequences later. Olivia had never given herself freely to a man, and she knew Logan needed someone to love him unconditionally more than anything. It might not be forever, but she'd do her best to give him what he needed now.

They drove in silence up the dirt road that wound through the hills outside of Telluride. Logan wanted to say something, really he did, but wasn't sure he trusted his voice at this moment.

Olivia wrecked him.

Of course he'd been lying when he spoke to Damien.

He could hardly breathe for what she meant to him. But how could he admit that? He had nothing to offer her.

Except this moment.

He pulled to a stop in front of the small cabin.

She turned to him. "Is this yours?"

"I had a little insurance money from when my mom died. Damien owned the land and gave me a great deal on a couple acres. I'd spent hours imagining a house of my own when I started doing construction work. This is how it turned out."

"It's gorgeous." A small smile played at the corner of her mouth. She leaned forward to take in her surroundings. "Thank you for bringing me here."

"Always so polite," he murmured and leaned across the seat to nip at her earlobe.

She let out a tiny moan and brushed her lips across his. "Kiss me, damn you," she said then giggled.

He laughed along with her.

"I'm not good at bossy," she said. "But I would like you to kiss me." She paused and added, "Please."

He was happy to comply with her request. He loved the feel of her mouth, the taste of her and her sweet, intoxicating scent. After a few moments she lifted her head. "Do you still have a roommate living with you?" Her eyes darted to the cabin then back to him.

"It was a temporary arrangement. The house is empty."

He forced himself to let her go, climbing out of the truck and around to her side. She'd opened the door but sat perched on the edge of the seat, her hands folded in her lap.

"Was it a woman?"

He raised his brows, not following her question.

"Your roommate," she clarified. "Was it a woman? Not that I have any right to…I'm simply wondering if…"

He stepped between her legs, into her space. Fisting his hands in her hair, he kissed her again before resting his forehead against hers. "It was a guy I knew from Albuquerque who needed help getting back on his feet after he landed in some trouble."

"Oh," she breathed. "Do you do that often? Take in people who need a hand up?"

"Sometimes. When I can and if it's someone I think I can trust." He drew his head back and ran his fingers across her face, easing the worry lines that creased her brow. "I've never brought a woman here, Olivia. I'm not a choir boy, but this place means something more. It's part of me and I haven't wanted to share it with anyone." He broke off, knowing that he'd revealed more than he wanted with that sentence.

Olivia wrapped her arms around his neck, bringing him close to whisper in his ear, "Until now?"

"Until now," he agreed and pulled her into his arms. She wrapped her legs around his waist and he kicked shut the truck's door.

He fumbled with the lock, then crossed the threshold. Olivia closed the door and Logan let her feet slide to the floor. He didn't let her go, couldn't make himself release her even when she squirmed. She turned in his arms instead and he waited as her gaze took in his home. It wasn't big or fancy, but somehow he'd poured all of his secret dreams into this space.

He tried to see the cabin through her eyes: The rough-hewed logs ran the length of the family room and the large picture window on the far side of the main dining area. He'd chosen neutral paint colors and large leather furniture. He didn't have many decorations, but he'd done his best to make the home comfortable and cozy.

"It's wonderful," she said on a sigh. "Every part of it is you, Logan."

She couldn't know how right she was. He'd spent hours scrutinizing each detail, from the knobs on the cabinet doors to the layout of the wide-plank flooring.

"Most of the materials are reclaimed from old barns and home sites around here. Although it's new construction, I wanted to make it feel like...it belonged."

Like I belonged, he'd almost said.

She wrapped her long fingers around his arms and stepped away from his hold, then laced her fingers through his as she walked toward the window at the far wall.

"You can see everything from here." She glanced up at him, then back through the large picture window. From this vantage point, the entire valley stretched out below. He'd based the whole house around this view.

He loved to watch the sun set over the mountains to the west of town, see the lights from the highway and the ski resort during the winter. But at this moment, he couldn't take his eyes off Olivia. Her perceptive gaze took in everything, even the things he thought he'd buried so deep no one could ever find them.

Gathering her close, he tipped her head back to kiss her mouth, then trailed his lips across her jaw and down her throat, humming against the pulse that beat against her skin. He unzipped her coat and she shrugged out of it, shivering slightly as he pulled her sweater over her head.

She turned in his arms and pushed his coat off his shoulders. Her hands reached under the hem of his flannel shirt to graze across his back.

"I want you here," he whispered along her skin and she nodded in response.

A soft groan escaped his lips as her hips moved against

him. "What the hell am I talking about?" he said on a laugh. "I want you everywhere."

She flashed a small smile and began to undo the buttons of his shirt. "You don't have to say anything," she reminded him. "This is enough."

She was wrong. It would never be enough with Olivia and that was the thing that staggered. Part of the reason he couldn't stay in Crimson was the memories that the town held for him. Little things such as a sound or smell could transport him in an instant back to the pain of his youth. But now the image of Olivia standing before him in the house he'd built would always stay with him. Already he could feel her permeating every inch of the cabin, the same way she'd subtly burrowed her way into his heart.

He sank to his knees on the couch, pulled her down with him, stripping them both until she was pressed against him. Then he was inside her, whispering her name like a prayer. She moved with him as if she'd known him for centuries, her soft cries tearing at the last vestiges of the walls he'd built around his heart.

"I never knew it could be like this," she whispered.

"Only between us," he assured her and had no doubt it was true.

He knew he'd never take in the view he loved without missing the woman he wasn't brave enough to claim as his own.

Chapter Thirteen

"I'd say she's well and truly in love with him."

The serving spoon Olivia held clattered to the counter. She picked it up, stirring the mashed potatoes in the pot on the stove as though she hadn't heard the words Sara Travers spoke.

"Can you blame her?" Natalie asked as she set water glasses on the big trestle table in Sara and Josh's kitchen. "He gives *easy on the eyes* a new definition, plus the way he looks at her..." Natalie gave a long whistle but didn't look up from her task.

Olivia felt her mouth open and close several times.

"They're just trying to bait you, sweetie." April Sommers patted Olivia's shoulder sympathetically. April helped out at Crimson Ranch when Sara was away. Sara had just gotten back from a three-day press junket for a movie she was starring in. She'd invited Olivia, Logan and Natalie out for dinner and to finalize the plans for the open house. The community center would officially open its doors next week, so this coming Friday was the event. From the feedback Olivia had gotten in town, most of Crimson was planning to attend along with several famous Aspen residents thanks to Sara calling in some favors from her celebrity friends.

"How does he look at me?" Olivia murmured, almost to herself.

"Like you're the only thing on the dessert menu," April answered with a smile.

"And he's got one hell of a sweet tooth," Sara called out.

"Oh." Olivia breathed out the syllable as heat filled her cheeks. Because that's the way Logan made her feel. Something had changed since that afternoon in Telluride. There was an urgency to Logan's touch, a need she could easily match but still wondered at. It was as if he was banking up their moments together, every touch and caress, to hold on to when he was gone.

"He's going back to Telluride after the opening," she said as Sara and Natalie came around the large island into the main cooking area.

"Really?" Sara took a pile of cloth napkins from one of the drawers. The ranch was closed for guests for a few more weeks so it was just friends there tonight. "I would have thought his plans might change given the two of you."

"There isn't exactly a *two of us*. It's not a relationship. He's here and I'm here but that doesn't mean…" She realized she was babbling but couldn't stop. "Has Logan said—"

"He doesn't have to say anything." Natalie waved her hand up and down in front of Olivia. "You simply ooze sexual satisfaction."

Olivia gasped and jerked her head toward the open family room beyond the eating area of the kitchen. Josh's daughter, Claire, sat on the couch next to Jordan Dempsey. The two teens went to school together and Logan had invited Jordan to ride out to the ranch with them because the boy's father was working late. It was clear that Jordan idolized Logan, and Olivia felt like she was making inroads on having him not blame her for his mom's leaving.

"Don't worry," Sara told her, following Olivia's gaze. "They've both got headphones on so they won't hear us. Chances are they're texting each other. Why bother speaking when your thumbs can do the talking?"

Olivia kept her eyes on Jordan for a few moments more, but all his concentration was indeed focused on the cell phone in his hands. She smoothed her fingers over her hair. "Can you really see satisfaction ooze? It's not a great mental image."

Natalie nodded but her eyes were kind. "It's quite nauseating if you must know. Between you and Sara, the happiness is almost overwhelming."

"You're jealous." Sara laughed. "But your time will come, Nat."

Natalie rolled her eyes. "I'm not looking for a man, ladies. I've got potato chips to keep me company and that's all I need."

Sara came back to the island and leaned toward Olivia. "You're in love with him," she said in a conspiratorial whisper loud enough so they all could hear.

The spoon dropped again, this time to the floor.

"Let me take over." April nudged Olivia to the side. "Sara, stop messing with her."

Sara's smile was unapologetic. "You do love him, right?"

"I've only known him for a month. I dated Craig for almost two years before either of us used the *L* word."

"That's because he wasn't your soul mate."

All three women looked to April, who was calmly scooping potatoes into a serving bowl. She just shrugged. "It's different when it's the right one."

Natalie let out a bark of laughter. "Or is it because her ex husband was a tool?"

April smiled. "There's that, too."

Olivia's head was beginning to swim. "I'm not..." She placed her palms on the cool granite of the counter. "It doesn't matter. He's leaving next week."

"Telluride isn't that far away," Natalie offered.

Olivia shook her head. "He doesn't...I don't...it wouldn't work." That much she knew to be true. Yes, she loved him. Even if she wasn't about to say the words out loud. There was no way she could manage a long-distance, casual dating relationship with Logan. Her feelings for him were too strong.

"I couldn't keep saying goodbye," she said after a moment.

All three women nodded. April patted her arm and Sara came around the counter to hug Olivia. "I'm sorry if I upset you."

"It's okay," Olivia answered. "I'm grateful for the time I've had with him."

"You're too nice," Natalie said. "Not that I have anything against a hot rebound relationship. At least you're not still thinking about your dirtbag ex-husband."

"Craig sent me an email last week." Olivia took the stack of plates from the counter to the table.

She saw the three women exchange a look.

"He wanted me to ship some of his clothes and stuff to

him." She looked over at Jordan to make sure he was still wearing the headphones. "They're in Albuquerque now."

"What did you do?" Natalie asked.

Olivia couldn't help the smile that played at the corner of her mouth. "Boxed everything up and donated it."

"Nice work." Natalie held up her palm and Olivia gave her a tentative high five.

"I think this calls for a toast." April pulled four wineglasses out of the cabinet.

Sara took a bottle of wine from the refrigerator and poured a bit in each glass. The four women held them up. Olivia's chest expanded at how nice it felt to finally have true friends in her life.

"To leaving the past behind," Sara said.

"I'll drink to that." Natalie clinked her glass against the others with a little too much force.

Olivia wondered what was going on, but before she could ask, the men came in from the back patio. The temperature had inched up several degrees over the past few days and it almost felt as though spring was coming again to the mountains.

"Steaks are ready," Josh announced, holding up a plate. His brows rose at the four women with their glasses held aloft. "What's the occasion?"

"Olivia threw away the cheater's stuff," Natalie supplied.

She felt Logan's gaze track to hers. She hadn't mentioned cleaning out Craig's closet to him.

"Atta girl," Noah told her. "Serves him right."

She felt herself blush and mumbled, "Thanks."

They all took their seats at the dinner table.

Logan was seated next to her and as he filled her water glass she whispered, "I'm sorry I didn't tell you about the clothes."

"No apologies, Olivia." His voice was tight. "You don't have to keep me apprised of what you do when we're not together."

"But still…"

He looked at her and his eyes softened. "I'm glad you did it."

She nodded, not trusting herself to speak.

"I stopped by the community center on my way in to town," Noah said from where he sat across the table from her. "The building looks great."

"Logan's done a wonderful job with all of the renovations." It was true, too. The painting was finished and the carpet had been laid yesterday. Furniture would be delivered tomorrow thanks to the most recent grant money that had come in.

"He told me the vision of the project was all yours. I'm sure the new mayor is excited about what this will do for the town."

"It's the least I can do for all the trouble Crimson has been through because of me."

"Because of your ex-husband," Logan corrected. "You didn't do anything wrong."

She bit down on her lip. "I'm happy to contribute, even so." She turned her gaze to Noah. "I hope you'll be here for the open house."

He nodded. "Wouldn't miss it. You should be proud of yourself, Olivia."

"Thank you," she murmured, pleased by the compliment.

Logan's hand inched up her leg. She glanced at him out of the corner of her eye but he was looking at Noah. His face appeared relaxed, but she could see a muscle knotting at his jaw. "I thought you were in the middle of a big project south of Denver," he said conversationally. "One that wouldn't let you get away so often."

His fingers began circling in a light rhythm on her thigh and she swallowed. Her stomach turned liquid and fluttery at his touch. When a small moan escaped her lips, she coughed to cover it up.

Noah sat back in his chair and focused his gaze on Olivia, ignoring Logan. "I'll drive up from the city for the weekend. Sounds like it's going to be a big event."

"I just got word from a couple of local musicians who've agreed to play that night." It was difficult to keep her voice steady with Logan's hand moving farther up her leg. "The main room may even be large enough to set up a dance floor."

Noah's smile widened. "Then I hope you'll save me a dance."

"Of course," she said but it sounded like a squeak. As discreetly as she could, she placed her hand on top of Logan's, trying to push it away. Instead, he linked his fingers with hers.

"Olivia, are you okay?"

Her head jerked as she realized Sara had spoken to her.

April leaned forward in her seat. "You look rather flushed."

"I think it's the wine." She pushed back from the table, tugging out of Logan's grip. "I do feel a little overheated. I'll step onto the porch for a few minutes to cool down."

Logan scooted out his chair. "I'll go with you."

"Not necessary." She shook her head. Being alone with Logan right now was the last thing she needed to help cool down.

"I'll go." Noah stood, holding up his plate. "I'm finished anyway and want to take in as much fresh mountain air as I can before driving back to the city."

She thought she heard Logan mutter something under his breath, but when she looked down he gave her a bland smile. "Would you rather go home?"

"No," she answered quickly. "I just need...a little space right now."

Trying to ignore her tingling skin, she took her plate to the kitchen and followed Noah to the back door.

At several different points in his life, Logan had felt the need to punch something or someone. On more than one occasion he'd done just that. He'd been quite the brawler back in the day, although not since returning to the mountains after his time away.

But never had he wanted to drive his fist into another man's face as much as he did tonight with Noah. From the time he and Olivia had returned from the porch, Noah had barely left her side. He'd even offered to help with the dinner dishes, ingratiating himself to all of the females in the house. After the kitchen was clean, the adults sat around the kitchen table playing cards. Logan had gone to sit with Jordan instead, trying to get lost in an Xbox game. Instead, he'd been painfully aware of Noah's every gesture toward Olivia.

Logan watched his friend smile and saw Olivia laugh in response. The musical sound travelled to him, assaulting his senses over the loud thrum from the video game.

So he couldn't have been more delighted when Noah announced his departure. Good riddance as far as Logan was concerned.

Then Josh crooked a finger at him. "Walk Noah out with me," he said from the edge of the couch.

"In the middle of a game here."

The sound of gunfire and yelling came from the TV.

Then it went quiet. "Dude." Jordan elbowed him in the ribs. "You died again."

"Hey, Jordan," Josh said, "Sara's cutting a cheese-cake in the kitchen. You might want to get a slice before it's gone."

"Awesome." Jordan dropped the game controller on the couch and stepped past Logan.

"Come on." Josh nudged Logan with his foot.

"There better be cheesecake left when I get back," Logan called to Jordan. "Since I made it."

Logan was still grumbling as he followed Josh out the front door.

Noah leaned against his truck, arms folded across his chest. "That was fun," he said with a smile.

Logan stepped forward with a growl, but Josh grabbed his arm. "Use your words, Logan. We're all adults here."

"What the hell is wrong with you?" he asked Noah as he shook off his brother's grasp. "You were practically drooling on Olivia all night. Like I wasn't even there."

"Back when she was married to Craig Wilder, I didn't realize how pretty she was." Noah tapped a finger on his chin as Logan's head started to pound. "No, that's not exactly true. I knew she was pretty, but she was so stand-offish. Plus she was saddled with such a loser. I didn't notice her like that." He straightened, rubbing his hands together in front of him. "Now I see how much she has to offer. She's smart, kind, beautiful…damn near the whole package. The kind of woman a man could just sink into and—"

Logan launched himself forward taking fistfuls of Noah's down jacket and pushing him with a thud into the truck. "Don't talk about her like that."

Noah pushed back. "Why do you care? You're leav-ing next week."

"I care because I…" Logan's voice trailed off as one side of Noah's mouth quirked into a knowing smile. He turned, took several angry steps down the driveway.

"You're leaving," Noah said behind him. "You have no claim on her that I can see. If another guy wanted to—"

"Noah, stop." Josh's voice was firm. "You're poking the bear too hard, my friend."

Logan drew in a breath, forced his fists to unclench. He turned, watching Noah smooth out the front of his jacket. "I don't want her to get hurt."

"As far as I can tell, you're the one who's going to hurt her."

"You're right." Logan ran his hands through his hair. "I have no claim on her. She needs someone who can give her the life she deserves. Despite the fact that you're annoying as hell, you're a stand-up guy, Noah. If you want to date Olivia after I'm gone, that's—"

"Shut up." Noah threw his hands in the air. "You two might be the biggest idiots on the planet. Did Jake get all the brains in the family?"

"I'm not an idiot," Josh protested.

"You were before Sara got a hold of you." Noah pointed a finger at Logan. "I don't want to date Olivia, you schmuck."

"Then what was that show tonight about?"

Noah shook his head. "It was about demonstrating that if you don't step up to the plate, someone *is* going to swoop in and take your girl."

"She's not my—"

Noah held up a hand. "Don't say it. It's obvious how you feel about her and she's clearly crazy about you."

"Or just plain crazy," Josh offered with a smile.

"Are you seriously going to tell me it wouldn't kill you to see her with another man?" Noah took a step closer.

"Because I was pretty sure you wanted to beat me to a pulp most of this evening."

"I'm leaving after the community center opens."

"You don't have to go."

"I can't stay in Crimson. You know why I can't be here for the long term."

"Logan, the accident was more than ten years ago. You can't let Beth's death define your life."

"She wouldn't want that," Josh agreed.

Logan closed his eyes for a moment to clear the red that was clouding his vision. "Don't talk about her like you know what she'd want. She'd want to be alive right now, not buried in the ground because I let her go that night."

Josh's mouth thinned. "The accident wasn't your fault."

"How do you know, Josh?" Logan pointed a finger at his older brother. "You and Jake got the hell out of that house and never looked back. Beth and I were stuck with dad. There was no one to run interference anymore when he got a bad drunk on."

"I'm sorry."

Logan shook his head. "I would have done the same thing. All any of us ever wanted was to get away. That's why I started making trouble, and Beth was drinking and partying with a wild crowd. It's why I lost my connection with her." He swallowed around the ball of guilt in his throat. "She was my twin sister. She was part of me. We were both too hell-bent on our own destruction to help each other."

"I *do* know how you feel. I spent years blaming myself for leaving the two of you. I'm sure it's what keeps Jake running to the ends of the earth. Hell, he looked panic stricken the whole weekend he was here for the wedding. We all made mistakes, Logan. But none of us is to blame."

"You don't know anything, Josh. She was my twin. I felt it when she died. The pain felt like it was coming from me, like I was the one thrown from that car wreck. It ripped me in two. A part of me was gone." He bent forward, doubled over with emotion all over again. After a few minutes, he looked up at his brother's concerned face. "Everywhere I go in this town, something reminds me of her. A smell, a sound. I can't keep the memories at bay. I see her when she was a kid, all the times we hid out in town or bummed a ride on the highway. Every single thing is her memory. Everything but..."

"Olivia," Josh supplied after a moment.

Logan nodded. "She's new and fresh. She helps me forget how much it hurts. She helps me remember what it's like to live without guilt and pain and regret commanding my entire life. But I can't stay here. I can't overcome it."

Noah took a step forward. "She could—"

"No." Logan held up a hand. "I won't ask her to leave."

He watched as Noah gave Josh a pointed look. "He's scared."

"I'm not—"

"Can you blame him?" Josh answered

"She loves Crimson."

"I'm pretty sure she loves you more," Noah said quietly.

"It doesn't matter. I don't trust myself. I don't trust that the darkness I felt after Beth died won't come back to consume me again. It's always there in the periphery, waiting for me to let down my guard. I did more than my share of stupid, reckless things back then. Who knows why I'm even still here? When Beth was killed from one awful mistake and I have years' worth of them piled up around me. It could happen again. I could lose control." He met Josh's gaze. "Like Dad always did. I won't have Olivia around me when that happens."

"You're a different person now. You were a boy, Logan. A terrified, hurt, immature boy. It's not the same."

"I won't take that chance," he repeated. "She's too important." He turned to Noah. "Keep an eye on her when I'm gone. Make sure she finds someone worthy of her."

Noah stepped forward. "I'm sorry about tonight, man. I wanted to irritate you. I had no idea—"

"It's okay. You understand now."

Noah and Josh both nodded. Logan watched Noah climb into his truck and drive off, his taillights glowing through the darkness.

Josh glanced at him. "Let's go back in."

Logan turned but Josh reached out and wrapped him in a quick brotherly hug. "It wasn't your fault, Logan. You do what you need to, but I'm going to keep saying that until you believe it."

"You could be talking for a long time." Logan felt pain wash over him but hugged Josh back. They both pulled away at the same time.

"Enough family bonding?" Josh asked, his smile gentle.

"I need cheesecake and a beer."

Josh laughed. "I like that combination."

A dog came barreling out of the darkness behind them. Two large paws hit Logan square in the chest, knocking him back a few steps.

"Buster, down." Josh's voice was a firm command. The dog dropped to all fours and ambled over to nuzzle against Josh's leg. "What are you doing out here, boy?"

Logan looked around but saw nothing outside the circle of light from the front porch. "He must have snuck out the kitchen door."

"All the food's in the house, big guy." Josh rubbed the dog's ears. "Let's see if I can pass you a bite without April and Sara noticing."

Logan laughed. "Good luck with that."

Olivia watched the two men and Buster walk back in the front door from where she stood in the shadows next to the house.

"We shouldn't have heard that," she whispered, wrapping her arms around herself to ward off the shivers that didn't come from the cold night air.

Natalie nodded but said, "It was hard to stop listening."

They'd taken Buster out back to do his business but the dog had taken off after a sound at the front of the house. She and Natalie had followed the gravel path around the side of the house until they'd heard voices.

"He's punishing himself for something he didn't do, an accident that wasn't his fault." Olivia took Natalie's arm. "I have to make him see that he can move past his sister's death. It was a terrible tragedy, but he's not the one who died."

Natalie's eyes were sad. "Sweetie, there are some things—some people—who are too broken to fix."

"You say that like you have personal experience."

Natalie shrugged. "I'm only saying that you can't help Logan if he doesn't want it. And you're going to break your own heart trying."

"I have to try to help him realize how much better of a life he deserves. He did that for me. I wasn't even sure I had any heart left until he came along."

"What are you talking about? You've got one of the

biggest hearts I know. Even when dirtbag Craig was still in the picture, you were kind and caring."

"I don't mean that." Olivia shook her head as if doing so might sift her jumbled thoughts into order. "I'm not sure how to explain it. After Craig left, I expected to be devastated and I wasn't. Don't get me wrong, I was humiliated and scared, but that's not the same. My heart didn't feel broken. It was empty. I really thought I wasn't capable of anything more. That all the times I'd seen my mom tamp down her feelings for the sake of her image had actually become part of the fabric of me."

"You aren't your mother," Natalie said softly.

Olivia took a shuddering breath. "I know, but I wondered if I was as emotionally frigid as her. I think that's part of why I took on the community-center project in the first place. I believed in it. I wanted to do something for the town, but I also needed to stay busy. That way I could ignore how much I couldn't feel anything. I could live vicariously through the happiness I brought to other people."

Natalie squeezed her arm. "But you couldn't feel that happiness yourself?"

"Not until Logan. He opened something up in me. He made me believe in myself and taught me it was okay to be who I am inside. He helped me discover my heart again."

"And you gave it to him?"

Olivia nodded. "I know it's stupid. But even though I knew I should be protecting my heart with him, I didn't want to. For the first time in my life, I wanted to feel everything. I still do. So even if it hurts me in the long run, I've got to try. I've got to give him the gift that he gave me."

"I don't know a lot of people who'd welcome heart-break into their lives."

Olivia let out a small laugh. "I'm not sure there's any other way to truly experience love."

She clenched her fists, realizing she could barely feel her finger tips. Spring might have been coming to Crimson, but the nights were still frigid.

"We should go in. I want to—"

"Take your man home to warm up in bed?" Natalie suggested with a smile.

"Exactly."

They walked toward the back of the house. "Just know we'll be here for you no matter how things turn out."

Olivia gave her friend a hug as they entered the house. "That means the world to me."

Logan stood in the kitchen next to Josh and Sara. He smiled when he saw her, although it didn't quite make it to his eyes.

She approached him slowly, linking his fingers in hers, then lifting his hand to her mouth and kissing his knuckles. He darted a glance at the others in the kitchen.

"Josh, will you drive Jordan home for us?" She didn't take her eyes off Logan.

"Sure," Josh answered.

"What's going on?" Logan asked.

Olivia looked over her shoulder at Sara. "Thanks for dinner. I'll call you in the morning."

Sara nodded and Olivia tugged at Logan's arm.

He followed her through the house then spun her to face him as the front door closed behind them. "Is everything okay?"

As he dipped his head to look into her eyes, his tender expression made her heart sing. For the first time in as long as she could remember, Olivia thought that things might just turn out the way she wanted them to.

"It's perfect." She brought her lips to his, kissing him with all the love she felt.

She pulled back after a few seconds. "I want you to take me home." She put a hand on her chest, hoping she could control her rapid breathing. "I want...I need you tonight."

Logan looked dazed but nodded. He fumbled for the keys in his pocket, dropping them twice before opening the passenger-side door for her. Olivia hid a smile as she slipped into the truck. Maybe she had as much effect on him as he did on her.

He felt as much urgency as she did if the drive back to town was any indication. They didn't speak but before she'd even shrugged out of her coat, he took her in his arms, peeling the clothes off her body and stripping down himself. His touch was urgent and primal. There was no finesse when he claimed her body as his own. Olivia reveled in every moment of it, in the feel of his skin against hers and the weight of his body as he pressed her down onto the sheets.

Still she didn't say a word until much later, when he was curled behind her and her breathing settled to a normal pace. She snuggled against him and whispered, "I love you, Logan. You don't have to respond, but I want you to know it."

He turned her, searched her eyes. His were unreadable in the darkness. "I don't deserve you."

"I love you," she repeated. "Sometimes that makes everything else fall away."

He opened his mouth and she knew he was going to argue. She didn't want anything to change this moment so she placed a finger against his lips. "Nothing more tonight," she told him, then added, "Please."

He gave a small nod and she rested her head on his chest, drifting to sleep to the rhythm of his steady heartbeat, hoping her love was enough to save them both.

Chapter Fourteen

Olivia looked up from her laptop as Jordan came barreling into the community center's reception area a few days later.

"Where's Logan?" he asked, his eyes darting around the room.

"He went to get a few last-minute supplies. What's going on?"

Jordan's foot tapped with nervous energy. "Nothing. I just need to talk to Logan."

"Is it about the open house? I hope you're planning on coming. Your dad is welcome, too. He should see all the work you've done. He'd be proud of you, Jordan. We all are."

Something flashed in the boy's eyes as he took a step closer to her. "My mom came back last night."

It was a good thing Olivia was sitting behind the desk because her legs suddenly felt like rubber. Her mind whirred with the implications of what Jordan had just told her. She felt shocked but, to her surprise, not angry knowing that her husband's mistress had returned to town. She tried to keep her focus on Jordan and what this meant to him. "Is she...did she say...I'm sure you were happy to see her."

He nodded. "She cried a bunch. My dad yelled at her. I'm not a baby. I get what it means that she was gone, but I know he wanted her to come home. We both did."

"Of course," Olivia answered numbly. "Your parents will have a lot to manage through, but I hope they can make it work. I understand how much you've wanted to have your family back together."

"Dad hugged her at the end of the night." Jordan flashed a hopeful smile. "They thought I'd gone to bed, but I was watching from the stairs. She hugged him back like she meant it. Something's changed in her. I can tell."

"I hope so."

After an awkward moment, Jordan added, "She didn't say much about your husband. Only that she realized what was important to her and how sorry she was to have hurt Dad and me. I don't know if Mr. Wilder is returning to Crimson. I kind of hope not. I think my dad wants to beat him up pretty bad."

"That's understandable." Olivia was amazed that her mouth kept forming words as her mind raced. "I haven't heard from Craig, but if he does contact me I'll do my best to keep him away from your father."

"I know you were married to him, but he deserves to get his butt whooped." Jordan's fists clenched. "I bet Logan would be happy to back up my dad in a fight."

"No one is going to be fighting, Jordan."

Olivia's gaze darted to where Logan stood in the doorway. The understanding in his eyes almost undid her.

"Why not?" Jordan's face flushed a deep red. "If it

wasn't for Mr. Wilder, none of this would have happened." The boy's chin jutted forward. "I wanted to blame you," he told Olivia. "But you're a nice person. Even my dad thinks so. My mom feels real bad about what she did to you—to all of us. Why shouldn't someone put him in place?"

"Fighting is never an answer," Logan answered calmly.

"Easy for you to say now," Jordan countered. "You're big and tough. No one will mess with you. But you got into lots of fights when you were younger. I've heard stories."

Logan took a deep breath. "That's true. I learned my lesson the hard way. You're a lot smarter than I was, Jordan. Remember that."

Jordan blinked several times, his chin trembling. "I just want things to be normal again. If Mr. Wilder's afraid to come back to Crimson, maybe my dad can forget anything ever happened."

Olivia's heart broke for this boy. She hated her ex-husband for the pain he'd caused and believed Jordan's mother needed to make up for the pain she'd caused her husband and son. But if she was willing to try, it was up to Jeremy and Jordan to forgive her. "Your parents won't forget. But sometimes you can learn from the bad times and then work to make your life even better. That's my wish for your mom and dad."

That's my hope and prayer for all of us, she added silently.

The boy turned to Logan. "You can't leave Crimson now."

"You're going to be all right, Jordan. Your mom and dad love you. If you need anything, I'm only a phone call away."

"You don't have to go." Jordan shook his head, then turned to Olivia. "Tell him."

She bit down on her lip, using the pain to block her unruly emotions from rising to the surface. As a child, she would have given anything for her father to come home to their family, no matter how much she'd been hurt by him. Olivia felt nothing for Melissa Dempsey, but she'd come to care for Jordan and desperately wanted his story to turn out differently from hers. "Come to the community-center party, Jordan. Bring your mom with you if she wants. If I can help ease her return to town, I'll do that for you."

Jordan gave a jerky nod. "Thank you." Without looking at Logan, he turned and ran out of the building. The front door slammed behind him, then a deafening silence filled the room. Logan stood as still as granite. Olivia rose, took a step away from the desk and then stopped, unsure if she could bear to touch him right now. No matter how much she longed to.

"You think I'm wrong to offer to help my ex-husband's mistress," she said softly. "But I made the offer for Jordan, not his mother."

A muscle clenched in Logan's jaw. "Does that mean you forgive her?"

"I don't know. Does it matter? I was hurt by what happened between her and Craig, but in a way she helped free me. We'll never be friends, but it's not my place to punish her. She can take care of that all on her own."

His gaze snapped to hers, his eyes stark. "How can you always be such a good person? I don't…"

His voice trailed off and he looked so alone standing before her, as alone as she'd felt just weeks before.

"You were the one who made things okay for Jordan

in the first place." She tried to smile but her lips wouldn't curve. "Maybe I'm only following your lead."

"I told you not to make me into a hero, Olivia. I don't fit the part."

"You're human, Logan. We all are. It's you who expects more of yourself. You shouldn't—"

"What if Craig comes back?"

"I'll deal with that when and if it happens," she said on a shaky breath.

"And if he wants you back?"

"He won't."

"He'd be an idiot not to."

"It wouldn't matter, Logan. Craig is my past. I'm moving on with my life. Building a future in Crimson is my priority now. This town is home for me. It could be yours to if you'd let it."

He shook his head. "If I could stay here, I would. I need you to know that. If I was strong enough to make it work…"

"You don't give yourself enough credit."

"I have to leave, Olivia. I'm going to take off after the party."

"So soon? You could try for a little longer." She hated that she was begging ,but the words just poured out. "If we take it slow maybe—"

He cut her off with a sharp glance. "We're way past slow. I'll pack my stuff tomorrow. I'm sorry."

She dug her fingernails into the center of her palms to keep from crying. "You should talk to Jordan before you go. The next couple of weeks are going to be a big adjustment for his family. He needs you."

I need you, she wanted to scream. But she'd never been able to use her voice to make her own needs known.

His head jerked in a nod. "I will."

He lifted his hand as if to pull her to him but ran it across his face instead. "I'm sorr—"

"No!" She practically leaped forward, then covered her mouth with her hand. "No apologies between us," she said when she had her voice under control.

He flashed a sad smile as he turned. Before he made it two steps, he whirled back around and reached for her. His kiss was hard, searing into her senses. He devoured her mouth as if branding her with his touch. She arched into him just as he pulled back. Without another word, he walked away.

Olivia sagged against the reception counter, wondering if that was the kiss she'd hold on to in her memories for years to come.

Instead he came to her later that night. She'd eaten dinner by herself, trying not to notice that the lights in the garage apartment had been dark. Of course she wondered what he was doing on his last evening in town, but told herself it was no longer any of her business. Still, she'd locked and then unlocked her back door at least a half dozen times before she went to bed.

In the end she'd left it open and, just as she'd been drifting off to sleep, she'd heard Logan's footsteps outside her bedroom. He'd slipped under the covers and pulled her to him, but neither of them had spoken. For her part, Olivia wasn't sure if she could say a word without bursting into tears. Their intimacy had been slow, sweet and almost wistful. He'd kissed her body, running his hands across her skin as if he wanted to memorize every inch. The tenderness had almost undone her, but she'd forced herself not to cry. She'd told him she would take what he was able to give and wouldn't ask for anything more, and she was determined to be true to her word.

Much later in the night, she'd fallen asleep in his arms

but woke alone in a cold bed. That was the end, she knew. All she'd wanted was to curl up in a ball and wallow in her sadness. She'd worried about her lack of feeling after Craig left but now realized what a blessing that had been. Living with a truly broken heart was going to be more difficult than she could have ever imagined.

Someone was in the kitchen. Olivia heard the refrigerator door shut as she put on the last dab of mascara. *Logan*, she thought as her pulse raced. Hours earlier, he'd told her he'd see her at the open house, but evidently he'd changed his mind.

Could he have changed his mind about leaving, too?

The thought had her hurrying down the stairs.

But it wasn't Logan who sat at her kitchen table, sipping a glass of lemonade and polishing off the last of her brownies. The ones Logan had made.

"Craig, what the hell are you doing here?"

Her ex-husband tsked softly. "Cursing, Liv?" He shook his head. "That's not like you. It must be what happens when you take up with a guy like Logan Travers. He's pulling you down to his level."

She stalked forward, grabbed the glass out of his fingers. "You're the one who brought me to my lowest point, Craig. I think you'd have realized that by now." Part of her was tempted to throw it into his face, but she dumped the lemonade into the sink. Turning to face him, she pointed to the back door. "Get out."

"This is my house, too."

"Not anymore. We're divorced. Finished. Done. You wiped out our bank accounts. I got the mortgage." She took a step closer. "Not quite a fair deal, but I've made it work."

"You're different," he answered, a hint of a smile playing at the corner of his mouth. "Feisty. I like it."

She grabbed her cell phone from the counter and began dialing. "I'm calling the cops, Craig. This is my home now. Not yours. I want you to leave, and if I can't make you, they can."

"Wait."

She jerked her arm away when he touched her wrist.

"Please, Olivia."

Something in his voice made her fingers pause. She looked up and met his gaze. All traces of a smile were gone from his face.

"I'm sorry," he said softly. "I messed up. I hurt you and I'm sorry. You didn't deserve to be treated that way."

Olivia's fingers clenched around the phone, but she didn't move. "You don't belong here, Craig. I know Melissa's gone back to her family. I assume that's why you're in town. Whatever you feel about her, you need to let it go. She has a son who needs her."

"It was a fling." He scrubbed his hands over his face. "A stupid, life-wrecking fling. I just felt so stifled in Crimson, in my position as mayor and…"

"In our marriage?" Olivia asked the question without emotion, surprised that she felt so little for a man she'd once thought she loved. Now that she understood what real heartbreak felt like, she knew that Craig had never truly had any hold on her heart.

"Being a politician didn't fit me. It was my father's dream. I should have been strong enough to stand up to him from the start, but I wasn't."

Olivia backed up to the counter and crossed her arms over her chest. She did not want to have anything in common with her ex-husband, especially something that involved mistakes made trying to live up to their parents' expectations. "Is this where the violins start playing?"

"Sarcasm, too? You *have* changed."

Her eyes squeezed shut for a moment. "Why are you here, Craig?" she asked when she opened them again. "It isn't for Melissa and I know it's not because of me."

"Are you really involved with Travers?"

"My life isn't any of your business any longer."

"Logan is bad news. Always was. Stay away from him, Liv. You could do a lot better."

"You don't know what you're talking about. People change. They grow up. Logan is a good person. He's been a huge help getting the community center renovations done. I'd be lucky to have him in my life." She drew in a breath. "But he's leaving for Telluride after the open house tonight. So your concern is neither appreciated nor necessary."

"Doesn't surprise me. He's not the type to stick around for the long haul."

"Spoken like one who has experience in that area."

"I don't want to fight with you, Liv. I'm here because of the community center."

She felt her shoulders stiffen. "You have nothing to do with the community center."

He shrugged. "I need to get on with my life. It's not going to be with Melissa—"

"And it's not going to be in Crimson," Olivia finished for him.

His eyes narrowed. "It is *my* hometown. But I don't want to come back. I have a line on a few job opportunities down in Albuquerque, but my contacts are up here. I need references, people who will vouch for me. My dad made some calls, but it doesn't seem to be enough."

"It's not my fault that you burned your bridges in

Crimson. You can't possibly expect me to help you."
When he continued to study her, Olivia felt her mouth
drop open. "You *do* want my help. Are you joking?"

"I'm in a seriously bad spot, Liv. People in town won't
return my calls."

"Why is that my problem?"

"It's not," he admitted. "But if you could throw a little
kindness my way, it would help me mend fences in Crimson. I want to go to the event with you tonight."

She managed to sputter, "No way," before Craig held
up a hand.

"Just hear me out." He stood and paced to the edge
of the kitchen before turning to face her again. "I need
a couple of the town council members to vouch for the
work I did as mayor. If they see me with you, that things
are okay between us and we're friends, it would go a
long way."

"We're *not* friends!"

"It's one night, Liv. One event. I know how good you
are at playing the part. You can make this better." He
ran his hands through his hair. "If I can't figure things
out down in New Mexico, what choice do I have but to
come back to Crimson?"

"You don't mean that."

He shook his head. "I don't want to, but if there are
no other options, my dad has offered me a job in his
company. Just until I get my feet back under me. I know
you've moved on and, for whatever reason, you're doing
it in this town. Speaking of that, I thought the plan was
for you to move back to Saint Louis?"

"Plans change," she said through clenched teeth.

"You're still an outsider in Crimson."

"I'm not—"

"I'm sure you're working to make yourself a place

here, to be useful. Useful is what you do best. It would be difficult with us both in Crimson."

"Are you threatening me?"

He sighed, all earnest contrition. "I'm asking— begging—for your help. Please, Olivia. I need you."

Olivia gripped the counter as her head began to swim. Those three words, *I need you*, brought back a flood of memories from her childhood. It was what her father had always said to her mother after he'd returned from one of his stays in DC, when they all knew he'd been with Millie and her mother.

I need you, Diana, he'd say. *I need you to stand by me*. Not I love you or I'm sorry for breaking your heart. Simply *I need you*.

Olivia hated that she'd grown up to be like her mother, so easily swayed by three meaningless words. She wanted Craig out of her life, out of Crimson, for good, but she was no longer willing to sacrifice herself to make that happen.

This was her home now. Despite what her ex-husband might believe, she wasn't an outsider any longer. "No, Craig. You don't get to need me anymore. I can't stop you from returning to town, but I'm not letting you back into my life. I belong here, and nothing you do can change that."

He looked as shocked as she felt that she'd finally stood up to him. It turned out having a backbone suited her. Feeling lighter than she had in months, Olivia turned and walked away.

Chapter Fifteen

"You're fidgeting," Natalie told her for the tenth time later that evening.

"I'm nervous." Olivia's hands fluttered in front of her stomach and she clamped them together.

"The whole night came together perfectly," Sara assured her. "Other than your rotten ex crashing the party. Explain again why we aren't having the guys throw him out."

Her friends flanked either side of her, as Olivia had instructed them from the moment they arrived. But Sara was right. The open house was a definite success. It felt as if half the town had come to celebrate the dedication of the community center. Artists and teachers milled about in the different classrooms, handing out program guides and flyers. The dessert table was filled with goodies from the local bakery and a trio of musicians played near the far wall. A few older couples danced before them, although Olivia had declined Noah's playful invitation to join them.

She took a calming breath. "If Craig doesn't get a job in Albuquerque, he may move back to Crimson. I don't want him to think his presence matters to me or that he has the power to scare me off in any way. Besides, it's not a big deal."

"If you say so," Natalie answered. She and Sara didn't look convinced. "What does Logan think about Craig being here?"

"I'm sure he doesn't care. He's leaving anyway." The truth was she'd been too afraid of losing control of her emotions to talk to Logan about it. She'd had a feeling her ex would still show tonight, even though she'd refused to help him. She'd texted Logan the basics of Craig's return so he wouldn't be caught off guard. He hadn't responded, which was probably for the best. Or so she told herself.

"Logan has been shooting daggers in Craig's direction all night," Sara said, a smile in her voice. "I'd bet my last dollar that he cares more than you think." She gave Olivia a small hug. "Right now, I'm going to find my husband and force him to whisk me out on the dance floor. We'll keep an eye on your two men and make sure they stay in their respective corners."

Olivia chocked back a horrified laugh. "I don't have *men* and they don't have *corners*," she called to Sara's back.

She glanced to the edge of the room where Logan stood speaking to Ted. The older man patted Logan on the back then shook his hand, grinning broadly. Logan had insisted on using local Crimson suppliers and subcontractors instead of looking to Aspen or nearby Grand Junction for help. The town's economy had bounced back from what it had been a few years ago, but she knew how much it still meant to have money and labor kept local.

A broad laugh drew her attention. "You've done a fine job here, Olivia." Marshall Daley, Crimson's mayor, walked over to her. "I wasn't sure you could pull it off, but this place has exceeded everyone's expectations."

Except Logan's and mine, she thought to herself. "I'm glad you're happy with the outcome," she said out loud. "The center will need support from the town as well as private funders to really be a success."

"Right, right," he said with a wink. "I should see about hiring you to help with all our fund-raising projects. You do have a knack for it."

"Told you so," Natalie whispered, nudging Olivia in the ribs.

She rolled her eyes but smiled at her friend. "Didn't you want to check out the dessert table?"

"Take care of her while I'm gone, Marshall." Natalie started to walk away, then said to Olivia, "I'll bring you a cookie."

"The tiles were a brilliant idea," Marshall said as Natalie disappeared. A crowd milled around a table near the front of the room with a banner that read The Crimson Center Tile Program.

Olivia had come up with the plan to sell ceramic tiles to be used in a mural for the entrance wall, each tile personally decorated for the buyer. Natalie had arranged for a local potter to donate the use of his kiln and Natalie was handling the design of the tiles. Throughout the night a steady stream of people had filled out forms for the tiles. The last time she'd checked, they'd already raised several thousand dollars more for the center, much of it in cash donations.

"I'm overwhelmed by the community's support tonight," she said honestly. "I wasn't sure some of them could overcome my involvement enough to see how necessary this place is to the town."

"Nonsense." Marshall waved off her concern as if he hadn't expressed the same one only weeks ago. "You shouldn't be held accountable for something that wasn't your doing." He switched his gaze to where Craig stood, talking to several members of the town council. "Unlike some people who seem to have forgotten how much trouble they caused around here."

"Are you angry that Craig is here?" Olivia had seen the two men talking earlier.

"Craig Wilder's as smooth as a greased pig, I'll say that for him. He's been spinning more tales tonight than you'd believe, telling anyone who will listen how sorry he is and how much Crimson means to him. It's still pretty odd to see him back in town."

"You have no idea," Olivia couldn't help but answer. "I don't hold a grudge against him at this point." She hoped her nose wouldn't start to grow. "We all need to get on with our lives."

"Like I said before, you always were too good for him." Marshall tilted his head toward Logan, who was now standing with Noah Conrad. "Seems like you've got a soft spot for the bad boys."

"Being a bad person and having a wild past are two different things, Marshall." She waved a hand around the room. "None of this would have happened without Logan's dedication and expertise. He's as much responsible for the community center as I am."

"Is that so?" Marshall scratched his chin. "I guess maybe a leopard can change his spots. Logan Travers is all right, although I still have my doubts about your ex-husband."

Marshall ambled off into the crowd as Natalie returned. She handed Olivia a small plate with a piece of apple pie on it.

"Uh-oh," Natalie muttered after a few moments.

Olivia turned to her. "What's the matter?"

Natalie pointed at her. "You're not eating the pie. No one can resist Katie's pies. Heck, I just look at a slice and my mouth starts to water. Something's wrong."

"I'm okay. I'm just thinking…"

"About Logan?"

Olivia nodded. "He's leaving tonight."

"No long goodbye?"

"We already had our goodbye. I'm not sure I could take anymore."

Out of the corner of her eye she saw Craig lean closer to the man next to him, point toward Logan and let out a harsh laugh. "Except I need to say one thing to him now."

She maneuvered through several groups of people until she was standing before Logan and Noah. An emotion she couldn't quite place, but looked a lot like panic, crossed Logan's face. Really? Is this what it had come to already?

"I'm not going to make a scene," she blurted.

"I didn't think you were."

He closed his eyes for a moment. When he opened them again, his expression was kind but distant. It made her want to scream.

"Craig isn't here with me," she said quickly. "I told him I wouldn't help smooth things over in town for him. I wanted you to know that."

"I got your text." He lifted his chin to scan the room. "But thanks for the heads-up. I think Craig and I will both do our best to avoid each other tonight. I hope you remember that you're a lot stronger than he ever knew."

Olivia bit down on her lip before speaking. "I...thank you for saying that."

An awkward silence descended over the trio.

"This is a great evening," Noah said, smiling at her.

"Thank you," she said quietly, a ball of tension clogging her throat. She made a show of glancing at her watch. "I should find Marshall. He wanted to make a speech and do the official ribbon cutting before people start leaving." She forced herself to look at Logan. "You should be up front for that. Without your work, we wouldn't be here right now."

"I'm not one for the limelight." He shook his head. "I want to talk to Josh, then I've got to get going. Besides, you would have found someone else if I hadn't been here."

She looked away when her chin started to tremble. No, she wanted to scream. She'd never find someone else.

"I'll help you look for Marshall," Noah said smoothly.

She saw Logan stiffen, but he said nothing.

She nodded. "Let's go."

Noah took her arm and they walked away. With each step, the urge to sink to the ground grew until she could hardly move forward. Noah kept her going with an arm around her shoulder.

"Think of rainbows and unicorns," he whispered to her.

"What?" She pulled back, her confusion over his words temporarily diverting the grief that pulsed through her body.

He flashed a boyish grin. "I just wanted to distract you."

"Mission accomplished." She couldn't help but smile back at him. "You're a good man, Noah."

"But not the man for you?"

"Apparently I'm a glutton for heartbreak."

A woman walking by caught her attention. "Speaking of gluttony in the best of all possible ways." She reached out a hand. "Katie?"

The brunette turned.

"Thank you so much for providing the dessert table for this evening." She smiled sweetly before her eyes widened a fraction at Noah. "Do you know Noah Conrad?"

"Of course she knows me." Noah wrapped Katie Garrity in a hug that lifted her off her feet. Olivia noticed that Katie's eyes closed in a way that almost made her seem like she was in pain. "We've been old friends since high school. How are you, sweetheart?"

"Fine as always," Katie answered, her smile strained. "I didn't realize you were going to be in town this weekend."

"I drove up just for the opening. Added bonus that I got a slice of your apple pie as part of the bargain. You know it's my favorite."

Katie's smile tightened so much Olivia thought her mouth might break. Noah didn't seem to notice. He wiggled his eyebrows and leaned close to Katie's ear. "I'd tell you I was working my magic on Olivia, but much to my shock and dismay, she won't go out with me."

"Smart woman," Katie answered.

Noah playfully chucked her on the arm. "I thought you'd be on my side." He looked at Olivia. "Katie knows me better than almost anyone else on the planet. She can tell you I'm quite a catch."

"I don't think that's necessary." Olivia placed a hand on Katie's arm. "He's joking, you know. We're not dating. At all."

"Noah's always good for a laugh." Katie dabbed at the corner of one eye. "My allergies are acting up. I'm going to get a tissue. I'm glad you like the sweets, Olivia. The community center has turned out beautifully." She turned to Noah. "Enjoy your weekend."

"Let's have lunch tomorrow." He tugged on Katie's long ponytail. "I miss talking to you, bug."

"Lunch," Katie repeated, her voice thick. "Sure. Text me in the morning." She turned and headed toward the bathrooms down the main hallway.

"Did you two used to date?" Olivia asked, still unable to put a finger on the vibe she was getting from the other woman.

"Katie and me?" Noah laughed. "No way. She's like my sister. I went out with one of her friends in high school." He shook his head. "We've always been just friends."

Olivia didn't know Katie Garrity well enough to argue with Noah. And she couldn't imagine the affable, easygoing Noah riling anyone's feathers.

"Olivia," Marshall Daley called from a few feet away. "It's time for the dedication."

"Are you ready for this?" Noah asked quietly as they made their way forward.

She nodded. "I wish Logan would come up front with me. So much of this is because of him."

Noah studied her for a few moments, as if he realized she was talking about more than just the building renovations. "I'm sorry things didn't work out for the two of you."

She thought about her time with Logan and forced her mouth into a smile. "No apologies," she murmured. "This is a celebration."

The crowd in the room turned as Marshall tapped on a mic one of the musicians had handed him. "I'd like to introduce the woman we have to thank for bringing this historic building back to life."

He tugged Olivia forward as people clapped. "Olivia Wilder has been a member of our community for only a few short years, but already she's an integral part of Crimson's future success. Olivia, tell us about the work that's been done to renovate this building and your plans for the community center."

There was more applause as Olivia took the microphone from Marshall. "Thank you, everyone, for your support this evening. As much as I appreciate Marshall's kind words, there are many people who were involved in the community-center project."

She scanned the crowd and found Logan in the back of the room. He gave a small shake of his head, as if he didn't want her to publicly recognize him. He was an expert at playing down the good he did in people's lives. Even though he was leaving, Olivia wanted him to share in this moment as much as she wanted her next breath.

"There's one man in particular who was critical to the success of this renovation. I'd like to take a moment to—"

She was interrupted by a commotion at the side of the podium. Without warning, her ex-husband made his way through the town council members on either side of her. He enveloped Olivia in a huge hug, and she felt his lips brush the top of her head.

"I owe you for this, Liv," he whispered. "You really are the best."

"Craig, stop," she said on a hiss of breath. "What are you doing?"

"Fixing my life." He nudged her to the side and leaned forward to speak directly into the microphone. A disgruntled murmur went up from the crowd, but Craig ignored it. He began to speak about his initial vision for the community center, the dreams he had for the building and what the renovation would mean to the people of Crimson and how grateful he was to Olivia for carrying on in his absence.

Olivia listened, dumbfounded, as Craig reframed her efforts, managing to cast her in a supporting role while he became the driving force behind the entire project. Her gaze swept the faces of the people listening, many of whom looked confused. Sara and Natalie were watching her with narrowed eyes. Natalie drew her finger across her throat in an angry slash, clearly telling Olivia to cut off Craig's fictitious ramblings.

She glanced at her ex-husband, and as much as she wanted to stop him, Olivia felt rooted to the spot where she stood. Standing to the side while someone hijacked her life, appropriated her voice for their own ends, was second nature to her. How could she make a scene? It went against everything she'd been taught her whole life.

She tried to find Logan in the crowd but there was an empty space next to Noah at the back of the room. Noah gave her a sympathetic smile and tilted his head toward the door. Logan was gone. Of course he wouldn't stand by while she let herself be humiliated once again.

He'd expected more from her than she did from herself. Fear and doubt had held her captive for most of her life. Olivia was finished watching her life from the sidelines. The past few weeks had taught her that she wanted to be an active participant in every moment, to experience the joy and the pain so she'd know what it felt to be truly alive.

Reaching forward, she grabbed the mic out of Craig's hand. "That's an interesting story you're telling," she said into the microphone, taking a step out of her ex-husband's reach. "Too bad it's total fiction."

He moved toward her, shock and disbelief warring on his face, but Marshall held him back.

Pushing aside her tear, Olivia looked out into the crowd. "Let me explain how things really happened…"

Logan saw the lights of a truck swing into the cemetery, but he didn't stand. Cold seeped into his jeans from where he'd been kneeling in front of his sister's grave.

A few minutes later, footsteps crunched on the snow. "Logan, what the hell are you doing?" Josh's voice called out in the darkness.

"Do you visit her?" he heard himself ask.

Josh stopped a few feet from the headstone. Logan didn't look up.

"A couple of times a year," Josh said. "I don't have to be out here to remember her. I think about Beth all the time, Logan. I know it's different for you, because she was your twin. But we all miss her."

"This is the first time I've been at the cemetery since her funeral. You know it's her birthday next week."

"Which means it's your birthday, too. Only you're acting like you're already dead. Like you don't deserve any happiness in this life. You've got people who care about you, Logan. Who love you. But you're ignoring them out of some misplaced honor for Beth. She wouldn't want this."

"I know." Logan straightened, meeting his brother's gaze in the light cast down from the stars. "That's why I'm here. At the event tonight I wanted nothing more than to go after Craig Wilder for everything he's done to Olivia. I wanted to hurt him, Josh. Then when he hijacked her speech… I haven't felt so close to losing control since after Beth's accident. It felt like Beth all over again where I was watching someone I care about get hurt and not being able to do a thing to make it right. I thought I was going to snap. I had to get out of there. It was too much. Being in Crimson is too much for me."

"You're not the same person you were at eighteen," Josh said softly. "You've grown up, Logan. We all have."

Logan gave a jerky nod. "I'm starting to see that. I was heading out of town but I can't do it. I may not deserve Olivia, but I can't leave her. And all the memories I've been too damn scared to deal with involve Beth. Our childhood. Her death. I know that if I want to really start a new life, I have to make peace with the past. I don't know if I still have a chance, but I love Olivia."

"I'd say she'll be willing to give you another chance." Josh took a step closer. "After you left, she took back the microphone and ripped into her ex-husband so hard he'll probably have scars."

"Scars?" Logan repeated the word in a daze. "Olivia did that?"

"She was amazing," Josh said with a nod. "She catalogued, in great detail, how Craig had deceived and betrayed both her and—in a lot of ways—the whole town. I don't think Craig Wilder will be showing his face in Crimson again for a very long time."

"Good for her." Logan couldn't help but smile. "I knew she was stronger than she believed."

"She also talked about your work on the community center and how you deserve a lot of the credit for the project's success."

Logan waved away the compliment. "It was nothing."

"Don't do that." Josh pointed a finger at Logan. "Don't play down what you have to offer. We all know how successful you've been in Telluride. You can do the same thing in Crimson. Stop letting our family history define you. If you want a future in this town and with Olivia, have the guts to claim it, Logan."

"You're right." He took two steps toward his brother, a knot of emotion unfurling in his gut. "Where's Olivia now?"

Josh took his sweet time glancing at his phone. "I got a text from Sara. After the event wrapped up, everyone was heading downtown to continue the celebration. I'm guessing Noah gave Olivia a ride. Or maybe one of the other guys. She's quite a catch." Josh raised one eyebrow. "If you know what I mean."

Logan reached out and grabbed Josh by the front of his jacket. "Where downtown?"

"The Nickel and Dime Bar." Josh pulled away, smoothing his hands over his coat. "Relax, Logan. I'm just giving you a hard time. She wants you, no one else."

"But why me?" Logan hated the emotion in his voice. It sounded raw and weak. "Do you ever think you don't deserve Sara?"

"All the time." Josh laughed. "I know she's too good for me. That's why I work hard every day to earn my place at her side. You're not afraid of hard work, Logan. You can make this happen."

"I've got to get into town." Logan was already heading for the truck. "She thinks I left her when she needed me the most."

"Hold on." Josh caught up to him in a few strides. "Do you have a plan for what you're going to say?"

Logan shook his head. "Not yet, although I'm guessing it will involve some begging and pleading."

"Sounds good to me," Josh said with a grin. "I just wish Jake could be here to see it."

"Spoken like a true older brother. Are you going to follow me into town?"

Josh rubbed his palms together. "I wouldn't miss it. Mind if I record the whole thing?"

Logan stopped midstep.

"Joking," Josh said quickly. "Only joking. I know you're at least three football fields away from your comfort zone talking about feelings. I'll go easy on you."

"Let me be clear." Logan looked straight into his brother's eyes. "This has nothing to do with easy. You can take a video and invite the whole town to watch for all I care. I'm going to get my girl, tell her how much I love her and hope to hell it's enough. And if it is, I want everyone to know that Olivia Wilder belongs to me. Is that clear?"

"Crystal." Josh tucked his keys back in his pocket. "I'm driving with you, though. I don't want to miss a thing."

Chapter Sixteen

"I thought this was supposed to be a celebration." Sara gave Olivia's shoulders a squeeze.

"I'm celebrating." Olivia picked the tiny umbrella out of her glass and waved it in the air. "My drink is blue. How could that not mean a celebration?"

Natalie plopped down into the chair next to Olivia. "It looks more like you're drowning your sorrows."

"No sorrows," Olivia said, shaking her head. "No regrets." She raised her glass. "A toast to the future."

Natalie clinked her beer bottle against Olivia's fruity drink and grinned. "It was way cool to watch you publicly eviscerate your slimy ex-husband."

"I didn't mean to go off on him so hard." Olivia grimaced. "I got caught up in the moment."

"And what an awesome moment," Sara added. "He deserved everything you said. I just wish Logan could have been there to see you in all of your glory."

"You were on fire," Natalie confirmed. "It was hot. Very hot."

Olivia couldn't help but laugh. "I have to admit it felt pretty darn good. Turns out being a doormat doesn't suit me after all."

"I'm glad you realized it," Natalie said.

"I finally feel like I belong in Crimson." Olivia placed her drink on the table. "I probably always did, but now I believe it."

"It's just like Dorothy in *The Wizard of Oz*," Sara said. "You always had the power but you had to learn it for yourself."

"How do you do that?" Natalie leaned forward and made a show of peering into Sara's ear. "You can find a movie reference for any situation."

"It's my secret superpower," Sara answered with a wink.

Olivia took a deep breath as some of the heaviness around her heart began to lift. Her friends were right. She hadn't felt like celebrating anything tonight. Not with how raw the pain of missing Logan felt. But she had learned that she was tougher than she'd thought. And even if her whole body ached, she was going to keep moving forward.

"I'm going to go out front for a minute and call Millie," she told her friends. "She texted earlier to see how things went tonight. I'd like to invite her back to Crimson. We have a lot of catching up to do."

"We'll be right here," Sara assured her.

Several people stopped her as she made her way to the front of the bar, a couple to congratulate her on the open house and several to ask about upcoming classes and events at the community center.

She stepped out into the cool night air with a smile

on her face, already punching in her half sister's number on her phone.

"You made a big mistake messing with me, Liv."

Her finger stilled on the keypad as she glanced up to see Craig standing in the shadow of the bar's green awning. She could just make out the glint of his angry gaze. His arms were crossed over his chest and he took a step forward.

She glanced back to the door then fully faced him. "You're the one who made the mess, Craig." Her voice was steadier than she felt. "I told you I wouldn't help, but you tried to take advantage of me. Again. I'm done letting people walk all over me, especially you."

"You humiliated me in front of half the town."

"Paybacks are hell." She pocketed her phone, not wanting to spend any more time near her ex-husband. "Good luck with the future, Craig. I think you're going to need it."

She turned to leave, but Craig grabbed her arm. "You can't let me hang in the wind, Olivia." He yanked her around, his face inches from hers. "I brought you to this town. You'd be nothing here without me."

Her mouth fell open, but before she could make a sound Craig was jerked away from her. She watched Logan drop him to the ground with a single punch. Her ex-husband curled into a ball, moaning loudly.

"I think you broke my nose," he said through his fingers. Slowly, he stood. "I should sue you for that."

"Do whatever you need to, but don't ever touch her again." Logan shook out his hand and turned to Olivia. "Are you okay?"

She nodded, dazed at seeing him standing in front of her. "You hit him," she whispered as Craig turned and stumbled off into the alley next to the bar.

"I'm sorry if you think it was wrong." He took a step toward her then stilled. "My reputation around this town isn't the greatest, but that part of my life is over now. I'm not the enraged kid I once was, always looking for a fight. But your jerky ex-husband has been asking to be laid out all night."

She whirled around at the sound of clapping behind her. Several people, including Sara, Josh and Natalie, stood in front of the bar. A quick glance at the windows made it clear that most of the other patrons were watching the scene from inside. All of them were clapping.

"We have an audience," she said, turning back to Logan.

His smile was sheepish. "That's the first time anyone has ever applauded me for punching someone. I know you can take care of yourself, Olivia. But I need you to understand that I'm in your corner. Always."

"Always?" Olivia put her fingers over her mouth, trying to keep from bursting into loud, embarrassing sobs.

Logan reached out a hand and pulled her against his chest, his strong arms enveloping her. Olivia didn't know if it was his warmth or the way he smelled but suddenly the emotional roller coaster she'd been on caught up to her. She sagged against him, trying to catch her breath as the tears came again.

"So stupid. I'm sorry," she mumbled. "Craig was acting crazy. And I didn't expect to see you and…it's just all too much."

He ran a soothing hand along her hair. "No apologies," he reminded her, nuzzling his chin along the top of her head. "And no one is going to hurt you ever again."

She tipped her head up and noticed that the others had moved back into the bar. She tried to give Logan a worldly smile. "I made mincemeat of him in my speech."

One side of his mouth quirked. "I heard."

"I'm sorry you left the community center thinking I'd let him take credit for our project. I want you to know I'll always protect you. Whether or not you want me in your life."

His head bent toward hers and he captured her mouth in a gentle kiss. "I want you, Olivia. I want you in my life and my heart—hell, sometimes it feels like you are my heart. I love you."

She drew in a shaky breath. "You do?"

"I love you and I'm humbled that you would stand up for me. I want to do the same for you. I want to keep you safe and happy forever. Until I met you, I was just going through the motions. You brought me back to life, Olivia. Everything I am and will be is for you."

"I love you, Logan. You make me want to be brave, to try new things and to be myself. I never understood that it was okay to just be me before you came along."

"It's more than okay," he said and kissed her again. "You're perfect, Olivia. Perfect for me."

She bit down on her lip. "But you don't want to stay in Crimson."

"I want to try," he told her. "I left the open house tonight and started driving out of town, but I couldn't leave. I couldn't leave you. You're my lifeline." He smoothed his palms over her face, wiping away the last of her tears with the pads of his thumbs. "I went to visit my sister's grave. I needed to make peace with my past in order to move forward."

"And you have?"

"I've started to. I hope that with your help, I can continue. I want a life with you more than anything. I was just too much of an idiot to realize that you're all that's important to me."

She flashed a smile. "I'm glad to see you've wised up. Because I'm not going to let you go so easy again."

"You'll never have to."

She wound her arms around her neck and he lifted her off her feet, kissing her until she wasn't sure where he left off and she began.

"Get a room," she heard Natalie call out of the front of the bar.

Logan put her back on her feet. "Are you done celebrating?" he asked with a smile.

She turned, pressing her body against his. Her hands cupped his face and she lifted on tiptoe to look into his eyes. "I've only started," she told him. "You're stuck with me now, even when I get old and gray and you're still hot. I'm yours forever."

"That goes both ways," he said and kissed her again.

"Hey, you two," Sara called. "What do you think about taking that mutual admiration society off of the sidewalk?"

"Good idea," Logan said and laced his fingers with Olivia's. He leaned down to whisper in her ear. "Right now, I'm more interested in a private celebration back at home."

Olivia felt a blush start from her toes and quickly color her cheeks. "That's the best idea I've heard all day," she agreed, knowing her future would be better than she ever could have imagined.

* * * * *

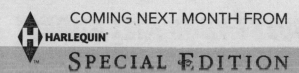
#2395 THE TAMING OF DELANEY FORTUNE
The Fortunes of Texas: Cowboy Country • by Michelle Major
Francisco Mendoza is having a bout of bad Fortune. Though he's been hired to help with the new Cowboy Country theme park, Cisco is told to lasso a member of the famous Fortune clan to help him out. So he courts spunky rancher Delaney Fortune Jones under the guise of helping him with his project...but falls for her instead! Can Delaney and Cisco find love in their very own pastures?

#2396 A DECENT PROPOSAL
The Bachelors of Blackwater Lake • by Teresa Southwick
When billionaire Burke Holden enters McKnight Automotive, he gets more than just an oil change. When beautiful mechanic Sydney McKnight asks him to be her pretend boyfriend, the sexy single dad happily accepts. But no-strings-attached can't last forever, especially since Burke's vowed to stay commitment-free. It might just take a true Montana miracle to give the Big Sky bachelor and the brunette beauty their very own happily-ever-after.

#2397 MEANT-TO-BE MOM
Jersey Boys • by Karen Templeton
Cole Rayburn's back home in Maple River, New Jersey...but he's definitely not a kid anymore. For one, he's got sole custody of his *own* two children; second, his boyhood best friend, Sabrina Noble, is all grown-up and easy on the eyes. Sabrina has just called off a disastrous engagement, so she's not looking to get buddy-buddy with any man...but it's soon clear that her bond with Cole is still very much alive. And he's not planning on letting her go—ever!

#2398 THE CEO'S BABY SURPRISE
The Prestons of Crystal Point • by Helen Lacey
Daniel Anderson is the richest and most arrogant man in town. He's also the most charming, and Mary-Jayne Preston falls under his spell—for one night. But that's all it takes for Mary-Jayne to fall pregnant with twins! The devastatingly handsome Daniel isn't daddy material, or so she thinks. As the mogul and the mom-to-be grow closer, can Daniel overcome his own tragic past to create a bright future with Mary-Jayne and their twins?

#2399 HIS SECRET SON
The Pirelli Brothers • by Stacy Connelly
Ten years ago, one night changed Lindsay Brookes's life forever, giving her a beloved son. But it didn't seem to mean as much to Ryder Kincaid, who went back to his cheerleader girlfriend. Now Lindsay is back home in Clearville, California, to tell her long-ago fling that he's a father. Already brokenhearted from a bitter divorce, Ryder is flabbergasted at this change of fortune...but little Trevor could bring together the family he's always dreamed of.

#2400 OH, BABY
The Crandall Lake Chronicles • by Patricia Kay
Sophie Marlowe and Dillon Burke parted ways long ago, but Fate has reunited the long-lost lovers. Sophie's young half sister and Dillon's nephew are expecting a baby, and it's up to these exes to help the youngsters create a happy family. Though the rakish former football player and the responsible guidance counselor seem to be complete opposites, there's no denying the irresistible attraction between them... and where there's smoke, there are flames of true love!

REQUEST YOUR FREE BOOKS!

2 FREE NOVELS PLUS 2 FREE GIFTS!

HARLEQUIN®

SPECIAL EDITION

Life, Love & Family

YES! Please send me 2 FREE Harlequin® Special Edition novels and my 2 FREE gifts (gifts are worth about $10). After receiving them, if I don't wish to receive any more books, I can return the shipping statement marked "cancel." If I don't cancel, I will receive 6 brand-new novels every month and be billed just $4.74 per book in the U.S. or $5.24 per book in Canada. That's a savings of at least 14% off the cover price! It's quite a bargain! Shipping and handling is just 50¢ per book in the U.S. and 75¢ per book in Canada.* I understand that accepting the 2 free books and gifts places me under no obligation to buy anything. I can always return a shipment and cancel at any time. Even if I never buy another book, the two free books and gifts are mine to keep forever.

235/335 HDN F45Y

Name	(PLEASE PRINT)	
Address		Apt. #
City	State/Prov.	Zip/Postal Code

Signature (if under 18, a parent or guardian must sign)

Mail to the **Harlequin® Reader Service:**
IN U.S.A.: P.O. Box 1867, Buffalo, NY 14240-1867
IN CANADA: P.O. Box 609, Fort Erie, Ontario L2A 5X3

Want to try two free books from another line?
Call 1-800-873-8635 or visit www.ReaderService.com.

* Terms and prices subject to change without notice. Prices do not include applicable taxes. Sales tax applicable in N.Y. Canadian residents will be charged applicable taxes. Offer not valid in Quebec. This offer is limited to one order per household. Not valid for current subscribers to Harlequin Special Edition books. All orders subject to credit approval. Credit or debit balances in a customer's account(s) may be offset by any other outstanding balance owed by or to the customer. Please allow 4 to 6 weeks for delivery. Offer available while quantities last.

Your Privacy—The Harlequin® Reader Service is committed to protecting your privacy. Our Privacy Policy is available online at www.ReaderService.com or upon request from the Harlequin Reader Service.

We make a portion of our mailing list available to reputable third parties that offer products we believe may interest you. If you prefer that we not exchange your name with third parties, or if you wish to clarify or modify your communication preferences, please visit us at www.ReaderService.com/consumerschoice or write to us at Harlequin Reader Service Preference Service, P.O. Box 9062, Buffalo, NY 14269. Include your complete name and address.

HSE13R

"I don't know why you're willing to go along with this but
I'm grateful. Seriously, thanks."

"You're welcome."

Oddly enough it had been an easy decision. The simple
answer was that he'd agreed because she had asked and he
wanted to see her again. Granted, he could have asked her
out, but he'd already have had a black mark against him
because of turning down her request. Now she owed him.

Sydney leaned against the bar, a thoughtful look on her
face. "I've never done anything like this before, but I know
my father. He'll ask questions. In fact he already did. We're
going to need a cover story. How we met. How long we've
been dating. That sort of thing."

"It makes sense to be prepared."

"So we should get together soon and discuss it."

"What about right now?" Burke suggested.

Her eyes widened. "You don't waste time, do you?"

"No time like the present. Have you already had dinner?"

She shook her head. "Why?"

"Do you have a date?" If not, there was a very real possibility that she'd changed into the red blazer, skinny jeans and heels just for him. Probably wanted to look her best while making her case. Still, he really hoped she wasn't meeting another guy.

She gave him an ironic look. "Seriously? If I was going out with someone, I wouldn't have asked you to participate in this crazy scheme."

"Crazy? I don't know, it's a decent proposal." He shrugged. "So you're free. Have dinner with me. What about the restaurant here at the lodge? It's pretty good."

"The best in town." But she shook her head. "Too intimate."

So she didn't want to be alone with him. "Oh?"

"Something more public. People should see us together." She snapped her fingers. "The Grizzly Bear Diner would be perfect."

"I know the place. Both charming. And romantic."

"You're either being a smart-ass or a snob."

"Heaven forbid."

"You haven't been there yet?" she asked.

"No, I have."

He signaled the bartender, and when she handed the bill to him, he took care of it. Then he settled his hand at the small of her back and said, "Let the adventure begin."

Don't miss
A DECENT PROPOSAL
by Teresa Southwick,
available April 2015 wherever
Harlequin® Special Edition books and ebooks are sold.

www.Harlequin.com

HARLEQUIN®

A Romance FOR EVERY MOOD™

Love the Harlequin book you just read?

Your opinion matters.

Review this book on your favorite book site, review site, blog or your own social media properties and share your opinion with other readers!

Be sure to connect with us at:
Harlequin.com/Newsletters
Facebook.com/HarlequinBooks
Twitter.com/HarlequinBooks

HARLEQUIN®

A Romance FOR EVERY MOOD™

**Stay up-to-date on all your
romance-reading news with the
Harlequin Shopping Guide,
featuring bestselling authors, exciting new
miniseries, books to watch and more!**

The newest issue will be delivered right to you
with our compliments! There are 4 each year.

Signing up is easy.

EMAIL

ShoppingGuide@Harlequin.ca

WRITE TO US

HARLEQUIN BOOKS
Attention: Customer Service Department
P.O. Box 9057, Buffalo, NY 14269-9057

OR PHONE

1-800-873-8635 in the United States
1-888-343-9777 in Canada

Please allow 4-6 weeks for delivery of the first issue by mail.

JUST CAN'T GET ENOUGH
ROMANCE
Looking for more?

Harlequin has everything from contemporary, passionate and heartwarming to suspenseful and inspirational stories.

Whatever your mood,
we have a romance just for you!

Connect with us to find your next great read,
special offers and more.

Facebook.com/HarlequinBooks
Twitter.com/HarlequinBooks
HarlequinBlog.com
Harlequin.com/Newsletters

www.Harlequin.com